SPIRIT

A DRAGON SOUL PRESS ANTHOLOGY

Edited by
J.E. FELDMAN

Editing & Formatting by Dragon Soul Press
Cover Art by Maria Spada

For those who crave incredible stories to wash away their troubles. New adventures are only a page away.

E.A. ROBINS

EA Robins is an American expat currently residing in South Korea. She began her writing career in 2019 with the publication of her first short story, *Hauntings*, in Of Metal and Magic: Compendium One released by the now defunct Fiction Vortex.

She spent the next year drafting her first full-length, fantasy novel, *Scion of the Oracle*, for a 2021 release date. EA is currently the social media officer for Of Metal and Magic Publishing, an epic fantasy, indie publishing co-op.

She hopes to one day master the processes of writing and publishing and to fill all future biographies with lists of her works.

Learn more at Facebook.com/RobinsWrites

THE BERLIN ASSIGNMENT

E.A. ROBINS

"The war is over," he says.

"Is it?" I ask, eyeing the rifle in his hand. It's polished clean, but worn, discolored by hard weather and harder use.

An almost imperceptible smile flickers across his thin lips. "He's not going to appreciate your sense of humor," he says.

"He never does," I say, slipping my hand behind my back.

His fingers tighten on the wooden stock of his gun. Even after all this time, even after surviving Stalingrad and taking Berlin, he doesn't trust me. The old doctrines are strong.

I set my weapon on the dented, steel table between us, a worn combat knife, its naked blade chipped near the base.

"I want it back," I say.

"No one wants your stupid finka knife," he says, looking at the weapon, but not touching it. With a jerk of his head he ushers me past his guard stand.

As I pass him, his face twists into a scream, blood flows from under his helmet, the flash from an explosion behind us lights his face, deepens its shadows. I can see his skull.

I avert my eyes and take a breath, letting the memory dissipate, unclenching my fists. There is blood on my palms.

The war is over.

Still, the city preserves its keepsakes. I reach out, brushing fingertips over the divots in the plaster of the walls, bullet holes and shrapnel scars. We all carry a few.

I pass the broken window. It's boarded up, but the silvery grey light from the street streams through in particle ridden beams. Midday. I push open the door to his office.

The KomDiv isn't alone. It takes him a moment to recognize me, another to take his hand from the revolver on his belt. He sighs.

"It is general courtesy to knock before entering," he says.

"Apologies, KomDiv. I was told you wanted to see me immediately," I say. "An urgent matter."

"Right, come in," the KomDiv says. He adjusts the fur and leather cap on his head. It's an ugly ushanka, but I've never seen him without it. "And shut the damn door, you're letting the cold in."

I glance at the other man in the room as I close the door and recognize him immediately. Not who he is, that's irrelevant. What he is.

The stranger meets my gaze and discreetly shakes his head.

"Your trip was uneventful?" the KomDiv asks, drawing my attention.

"Uneventful," I say.

That little Nazi resistance won't trouble you again, commander. You're welcome.

"You were gone longer than expected," he says, picking up a missive from his desk and reading it over as he waits for my response.

"A necessary delay," I say. "I continued onto Krakow to make sure the message was received."

Those S.S. bastards had been surprisingly good at covering their tracks across the Polish countryside. But, in the end, they got what they deserved.

The KomDiv grunts. He's accepted what I have and have not told him. This is as much of a debrief as I will get. He doesn't want to know the details.

"This is the specialist I was speaking of," the KomDiv says to the stranger, watching as I move toward the side table he uses as a bar cart.

"She is small for a shifter," the man says in French.

His voice holds just the right amount of disgust and the softest whisper of fear. I almost applaud. As if he does not reek of his own kind.

"Oui," I say, sipping the substantial drink I've poured myself. "Je suis le petit *shifter.*"

The KomDiv's mouth turns up in the ghost of a smile though he is not truly amused. He is an old man and this war is his last. The blockade tries his patience. The sneaking and spying and slitting of throats in the dark is not to his taste. It turns shadows into assassins and the whisper of the wind into the promises of the dead. There is a loaded mauser and a bottle of whisky in the bottom drawer of his desk.

"What do the French want?" I ask.

"Many things we will not give them," the KomDiv says. "But, Jean is not their envoy."

I regard the man, looking for more than was obvious as first. He is tall and slim, dark, and in possession of the fine high nose that afflicts those of Western European descent. He looks French to me.

"I don't understand," I say.

Jean smirks.

"The blockade is compromised," he says. "Supplies are still being flown in at Tempelhof and Gatow. And the new airfield they've constructed at Tegel is equally efficient. All told, there's a landing roughly every three minutes."

"And what can we do?" I ask looking toward my commander.

"If we can destroy the supply lines, and hold the airfields long enough for winter to set in, it's possible the Americans will leave Berlin," the KomDiv says. "Once they abandon the city, the British and the French will not remain."

"Destroy supply lines?" I ask. I shake my head. "Demolition is not my area of expertise."

"No," the KomDiv says. "But, it is Jean's. Now that you are here, you can take care of the GCA operators so that he can focus on the landing strips."

"GCA?" I ask, frowning.

"Ground-control approach," Jean says. "It's a radar system."

"For guiding in planes?" I ask. "That's rather clever. Helps them through this fog?"

"Mostly, yes," Jean says. "They've had some luck."

"Jean will see you through the barricades and put you in touch with the team that manages the Tempelhof system," the KomDiv says. "They're the best at what they do. If they are removed, there will be no one to replace them immediately."

"When do we leave?" I ask, setting down my empty glass.

"Now," Jean says. He picks up his coat from the back of a chair and an envelope from the KomDiv's desk. He tucks the missive into an inner pocket.

He has a hand on the heavy door when the KomDiv calls to us.

"You've got two days," the KomDiv says. "You won't want to be in that sector come Christmas."

I salute the KomDiv and turn to find Jean watching me. He has deep brown eyes and long, lovely eyelashes.

"Comrade," he says, tilting his head and stepping aside to allow me first departure.

OUTSIDE, THE DETRITUS OF THE CITY CRUNCHES UNDER MY thick boots. The streets have been swept, but there is nothing yet to clear the massive piles of rubble or mend the missile-sized holes that riddle the metropolis.

Jean leads me west, toward the barricades. I catch sight of the concrete blocks and barbed wire before he turns down an alleyway little wider than his shoulders. We duck under fallen boards and through a hole blasted in the back wall of a deserted building. I pause, looking back toward the street and when it seems no one has noticed us, I follow.

Halfway up the inside stair the building shakes, the explosion is deafening. The structure sways and gives way. Chunks of mortar rain from the upper stories. Someone screams and a severed limb lands on the step in front of me.

"Are you coming?" Jean asks, steady on the second-floor landing.

I nod, not daring to speak. He watches me for a moment, and then disappears through a doorway. I put a hand on the wall, forcing myself to take slow, deep breaths. The blood is gone. The war is over.

He's waiting for me in a small, intact room. Two empty wooden crates are set near a window, a metal bucket between them. The floor is covered in dust and the scattered remains of a newspaper, the print faded. Jean bends down and picks up a few of these scraps and a few pieces of wood from a pile in the corner. He tosses these into the bucket.

The single, unclean window faces west, and pressing my forehead to the cold glass, I can just make out the blurry forms.

"They have a tank," I say.

Jean is crouched over the bucket, striking a match. He shrugs.

"Then we will not go that way," he says.

When the fire is lit, he disappears for a moment, returning with a dented kettle. Using a rusted, metal spoon, he hangs it in the pitiful flames. After a few moments, I catch the faint scent of coffee.

He hands me a steaming mug and steps over to the window. He moves with confidence and grace and for a moment, I see him, the real him. The proud creature inside the human form. He senses my attention and turns, regarding me with piercing understanding.

"I'd thought you'd all gone into hiding," he says. "What brought you into this war?"

I hear the whistle of mortars, and pain, like a bullet, rips through my chest. I look into the depths of my coffee cup, unable to breathe. My vision darkens. My hands begin to shake and coffee spills over my fingers. It's hot, like blood.

"I followed someone," I finally say. Despite the steadiness of my voice, the depth of the wound is evident.

"I am sorry for your loss," he says, dropping his eyes.

"We've all lost," I say, setting my cup on the ground. "What of you? How does a French stag find his way to the ranks of the Red Army?"

"A long, sad story," Jean says and drinks from his mug. "In the end, our friends found me."

Our friends. Though we are not familiar, Jean and I are brethren, children born of the violent recruitment strategies the KGB reserved for serviceable shifters. Those who resisted were butchered and dumped in shared, unmarked graves. Those who submitted, reemerged, loyal and lethal, Stalin's most secret soldiers.

"How long has it been since you were yourself?" I ask,

considering the size of a mature buck. He would never go unnoticed in Berlin.

"Too long," Jean says. "As you observed, the KomDiv is meant to be kept unaware of my…"

He waves his hand in the air, searching for the word, before saying, "… spirit."

So, Jean has been set to watch the old man. Perhaps to ensure the putsch into East Berlin is successful. There is a twinge of pity in my breast, but it winks out upon recognition.

The silence condenses between us as the room fades into deeper shades of grey. It is not an uncomfortable quiet.

Finally, Jean says, "It's time."

We head south, keeping the blockade and its guards on our right until Jean bolts for the wreckage of a subway entrance and disappears.

He's standing a few steps down when I catch up to him. My eyes adjust faster and I continue down until I see a sign on the wall. I can't read it in the dark.

I hear Jean come up behind me and a faint metal click produces a small, flickering light.

"The North-South tunnel?" I ask, turning around. "It's flooded."

"Not all of it," Jean says, letting the lighter die and putting it back in his pocket. We don't need it. Using our inner beast to see through the blackest night is standard training. My eyes adjust again and we move on.

———

"SHE WILL TRAIN WITH YOU FOR TWO WEEKS. THEN REPORT back at Tegel," Jean says. His shoulders are squared, his beret tucked under his arm, stiffly holding out a plain, brown envelope. He is every inch the French sergeant that the patch on his uniform suggests.

We are standing in the entryway of a subterranean room, a gathering place for off-duty radar teams. A cold draft whistles through the cracks in the wooden door behind us. The space has a strange, but not disagreeable, muskiness.

"We've heard nothing about it," a man with a head of spiky red hair says, taking the envelope. He blocks my view of the rest of the room. His arms, the size of tree trunks, are crossed over his wine-barrel chest. I'm hoping he's not part of my assignment.

"I can't read this," he says, shoving the papers at Jean's chest. "We need them in English."

"These are what I have," Jean says, setting the beret back on his head. "It's been arranged."

"Oh, no. You're not leaving," the big man says, reaching out to grab Jean's shoulder before he reaches the door.

Jean jerks out of the man's grasp and turns, fists raised as he flows into a boxer's stance.

The big man smiles and pushes the sleeves of his shirt up to his elbow. He's in civilian clothes, and his breath smells of beer and garlic.

I take a few steps backward, until I can feel the wall. If this is going to be a fair fight, Jean won't have a chance.

"Woah. Easy, Harris," a woman says as she steps around the brute. She puts a hand on his arm and holds the other up toward Jean. "War's over. No need to start another one."

Sofia. My knees weaken. I grasp at the wall and a nearby chair to keep from falling.

There is a roaring in my head, the metallic grinding of a tank rolling over bodies, masking the sound of bones being crushed. *Sofia. How are you here? You're dead.*

Beautiful, undead Sofia, takes the crushed envelope from

Jean. She glances at the orders she cannot read and hands them to Harris.

And, I see it in the way she moves. This is not Sofia. This one's hair isn't as bright. Her eyes the blue of a frozen lake, not the grey of twilight. Her angles are sharper. Her nose bigger, once broken. This one is harder, muscles and discipline. Sofia had been smiles and soft, warm arms.

"Are you alright?" the woman who is not Sofia asks. "You look a little pale."

When I do not answer, she looks at Jean and asks, "Is she alright?"

"Je vais bien," I say. "I am fine."

"This is Lieutenant Brooks," Jean says. There is an odd intensity in his eyes. He wants me to recognize something, but I am at a loss. What have I missed? "You will report to her while you are here."

"Good to have you aboard," Lieutenant Brooks says, holding out her hand. I am slow to take it, hesitant to touch her.

When I do, it becomes clear what Jean was trying to get me to notice. She is one of us. She is a shifter.

I see the creature inside of her, and it is familiar and yet strange. Feline, but larger than any I've ever met.

On her part, Lieutenant Brooks gives no sign that she recognizes us. Her handshake is firm and professional.

"We've got it from here, sergeant," she says.

Jean salutes and departs without so much as a glance my way.

⸻

"We have twenty-four hours until our shift," Lieutenant Brooks says as she takes a stool at a long bar against the back wall. She motions for me to take the other.

"Then it's a brutal ninety-six on, which we work in paired rotation, until we're relieved."

"So relieved," the big man, Harris, says as he reaches between us and takes six bottles of beer off the counter, three in each hand. He winks at me and returns to his table. The rest of the team sits there. Two of them have women on their laps.

"How's the new strip at Tegel?" Lieutenant Brooks asks as she takes two more bottles from a wooden crate on the bar. "Have the new landing patterns been worked out?"

I try to speak, but have to clear my throat. I've been staring. I can't shake Sofia. The memory of our last kiss presses itself to my lips. Her crooked smile surfaces in my mind. Her warm body twists under my hands. The blast that split her into less than these pieces is deafening.

The beer is cold and bitter and clears my mind. Lieutenant Brooks is no longer my lost love.

Just as I begin to answer her question, the door to the basement opens, allowing a fierce gust of wintry wind into the space.

"Shut the door!" someone says.

The woman who's come in is wearing a dress coat, low heels, and bright red lipstick. A thick scarf is wrapped around her curled hair. She puts her hand on an empty chair as if she needs it to steady herself.

With a broad, white smile, she says, "They're here."

Someone groans. Chairs are pushed back, away from tables. Lieutenant Brooks smiles and claps me on the back.

"You're in for a treat," she says. She drinks the rest of her beer in a long pull.

"What's going on?" I ask as we join Harris and the others, pulling on coats, scarves, and thick caps.

Specialist Brooks burps lightly into her hand as Harris hands me a pair of heavy work gloves.

"Special assignment," he says.

"These aren't mine," I say, trying to hand them back.

He shakes his head and says, "You'll want them."

"Let's shake a leg," Lieutenant Brooks says, pulling open the door. "Don't want to be late."

I pull on the gloves as we move outside. It smells like snow. It'd be the first of the winter.

The team seems to be in a good mood. They joke with each other, and call out greetings to the few people we pass. I let myself trail behind them. I haven't forgotten why I am here.

There's five of them. Too many to take at once. Harris is the largest by far, but even Lieutenant Brooks is larger than I am. And though they all move with the confidence of fighters, she's the one that concerns me.

As if my thoughts called to her, she turns and looks at me for a moment.

After a few more blocks, I can hear noise and see a bright light, though it's source is hidden around a corner. There are more people here and they are all moving in the same direction.

We come to an intersection that opens up in one quarter to a large plaza. Bonfires burn around the perimeter and in the center, next to the bottom half of a broken bell tower are several open back convoy trucks. There is a crowd of people surrounding these trucks.

As we approach, two men hop on the bed of one of the trucks and lift what appears to be a bound evergreen tree. They hand it down to those who are waiting.

The radar team is greeted by the men and women moving the trees and absorbed into the task. Harris takes one of the smaller trees on his shoulder and points to one of the waiting people.

"You," he says. "Show me the way."

The children shift, glancing at each other. One of them giggles nervously.

"Have I got something on my face?" Harris asks, crossing his eyes and touching his nose.

A wave of smiles breaks across the group. The giggles this time are true.

"Or..." Harris says, pulling the bag from behind his back and holding it high. "Is there something here that you want?"

The children have gone dreadfully quiet with expectation. One of them steps forward, a boy, his light hair cut short. The others divide their attention between him and the bag swinging from Harris's hand.

"Merry Christmas, sir," the boy says in English.

There is a moment of silence. And then Harris grins.

"That it is, little ones!" he says, reaching into the bag and drawing forth candies wrapped in shiny paper. "Wiggly Wings isn't the only one handing out candy tonight!"

The children surge forward, babbling in German and broken English. Their small hands held toward the treats that Harris deals out as if he were some giant, red headed Santa Claus.

When the bag is empty, the children retreat, holding their sweets like gold in their gloved hands.

"It's going to be busy?" I ask, sipping the whiskey we've been drinking.

Upon our return to the break room, a fresh box of beer and spirits had been discovered, set on the table in the middle of the room. Lieutenant Brooks had set most of it aside for the other teams, but the bottles kept out had served their purpose.

"Well, of course it is," she says. She speaks low and slow,

like a drunken cowboy. Every vowel is drawn out in her heavily nasal accent. It's intoxicating in a way the alcohol can't match. I want her to keep talking.

"Rations and fuel might be a bit light this year," she says. "But we're going to make sure that no one goes without this Christmas. Right, boys?"

There's a chorus of agreement from the team. They sit, playing cards near the wood stoves. Candles burn in clusters around the space. It's warm and merry in this little den.

"I'd like to ask you a question, Lieutenant Brooks," I say.

"You don't have to call me that," she says.

"Excuse me?"

"My real name is Barbara," she says. "But no one calls me that. The guys will only call me lieutenant, but you can call me Bobby."

"Bobby," I say and she smiles at me.

It suits her. The name, and the smile.

"You're staring," she says.

I clear my throat, dropping my gaze to the table. "They, ah. They know...what you are?" I ask.

She blinks. I've startled her.

"I've heard the French are forward, but you're something else," she says with a laugh. It is a good laugh, and it softens her sharpness.

"I didn't mean to be rude," I say, looking down again into my glass. There's just a bit of the amber liquor in the bottom. It catches the light and sparkles.

"Before this assignment, Harris and I were in Belgium," Bobby says. She picks up the bottle and freshens my glass. "There was a bit of a sticky situation in the Ardennes. We were foxholed. They kept charging up the hill. I'd run out of ammunition..."

She shrugs and says, "I did what I had to do. After, I was reassigned. Captain wouldn't even look at me."

She takes a drink directly from the bottle before tipping it into her cup. Then, she turns around, setting her elbows on the bar and watching her team playing cards.

"When it was all over, and most were getting shipped home, those four petitioned to stay," she says. "Found me in Monmouth training on radar. Turns out, they've got a knack for it."

There is a warm, nostalgic smile on her face. The whiskey has colored her cheeks and brightened her eyes. She's almost pretty in the half light of the wood stove.

"What are you?" I ask, almost in a whisper.

She isn't surprised this time. She turns her head, regarding me. All of me. Her eyes drip over my shoulders and down the lines of my body. She angles her chin and stares into my eyes.

"I'm like you," she says.

And I know. I can see it all in her eyes. The blue of skies over bare rock mountains, stalking swift prey under always green pines. The scent of the wind with no trace of man. The deep comfort of a den, made warm by your mate.

I drop my eyes. I know my cheeks are flushed, but there is nothing I can do. She's twisted the insides of me with the direct intensity of intimate desires.

She seems to remember herself, and she, too, averts her gaze.

"I'm cougar clan," she says.

When I don't respond, she looks up again and says, "Mountain lions."

"Merry Christmas Eve!" Harris says as he joins us, interrupting whatever Bobby was about to say. He throws an arm over her shoulder and pours from his bottle into my already full cup. "Drink it while you got it. For tomorrow, we land some planes."

"Tonight," Bobby corrects him.

Harris groans and says, "Right. Right. We'll be ready. Let the Reds try it!"

Someone starts singing a slurred Christmas song and Harris's face lights up. He turns away, joining in at a bellow.

"Try it?" I ask.

"There's been a rumor the Russians are going to make a push east," Bobby says. "Was meant to be late summer, then in the fall. Now, it's Christmas."

"No credit to it?" I ask, thinking of the KomDiv and his master plan. And the part I'd been tasked to play.

"Not yet," Bobby says.

Harris returns then, still singing and grabs us both by the arm, pulling us toward the off-key choir and spilling drinks.

THE OTHERS ARE TALKING QUIETLY AND SMOKING BY THE WOOD stove, nursing the last of the whiskey. Harris lays across a table, snoring and grunting in his sleep. The candles have burnt themselves out.

Bobby and I sit in a darker corner, our backs against the wall, empty glasses on a table between us. She takes a long drag of her cigarette and then passes it over to me. I close my eyes, more relaxed than I have been in a long time. More than I have any right to be in this moment.

I take a drag of the cigarette and then, frowning, stare at its bright ember. There hasn't been any bombs or blood in my head in hours. Not since I first mistook Bobby for Sofia.

I look over at the lieutenant and find she is watching me.

I hand the cigarette back to her as she asks, "How long has it been?"

"Not so long," I say, thinking of my previous assignment.

The expression on her face reminds me of who I am

meant to be. I cough, trying to cover the slip with a farce of embarrassment.

"I mean, I know I'm not supposed to, but…"

"I do it sometimes, too," Bobby says. She's leaned in, across the table. "Sometimes, I climb up onto the roof at night and just sit there."

She closes her eyes and leans back in her chair, saying, "The wind in my fur…"

The room settles into silence. The fire has died down to glowing red coals. The men around it, slumped in their chairs, breathing heavily. Bobby sits so still, I think she, too, is sleeping.

I look at her pale, exposed neck. This is the time.

I lean forward, careful not to allow my chair to creak, and reach back, under my jacket. I close my fingers around the hilt of my knife and then I pause.

There is a warning in me, a sudden certain knowledge. That if I do this, I will always be doing this. She will be the first of many undeserved deaths.

I lean forward, dropping my head into my hands.

She stirs as I reach for my coat.

"Where are you going?" she asks.

"I need some air," I say. I can't stay. I head for the door, but she stands and catches my hand.

When I don't pull away, she slips her fingers between mine. Her cautious smile is kittenish, shy and inviting.

"Come with me," she says.

She pulls me toward the back of the room, through a door, and up a set of crooked stairs. She glances back at me as we walk through the shadowy grey rooms of a forsaken home. The fragments of abandoned lives still hanging from the walls, sitting on the tables. Another staircase and through the doorway at the end of the hall.

This last set of stairs is more of a ladder, but opens up to a great, wide room, the length and breadth of the house. There are piles of boxes, things covered with sheets, but it's brighter in here than an attic should be.

Behind me, there is a great, round window. It's as tall and wide as my arms spread apart and looks out over a canal and the roofs of the apartments on the other side. The city is black. The blanket of clouds less so, glowing with the unfettered celestial light above. I'm drawn forward, the depth of night calming me.

"The team doesn't like it when I got out at night," Bobby says, moving to the edge of the window and running her hand along its curve. "So, this was the compromise."

Something clicks, and the great glass window swings inward.

The night air washes over me in a freezing wave. It's harsh and purifying. I take a deep breath in through my nose. Berlin sleeps, but I can hear the distant thrum of aircraft heading for the Templehof fields. Without the constant effort of the allied powers, this half of the city would soon be hungry and grow cold. They'd welcome the KomDiv, all the officers of the East, as long as they came bearing food and fuel.

After some time, I hear the rasp of a match against sandpaper and smell a faint wisp of sulfur.

I turn to find her standing naked in the candlelight. Her body is ripe in maturity, full and gentle in the flickering glow. She's half-shifted. I can see the outline of her small, erect ears. The shadow of her long, thick tail moving slowly behind her, held just above the floor. Her eyes are golden, bright, even in the darkness.

My breath stops in my chest. All I can manage is a soft, "Oh."

A smile tugs at the corner of her mouth.

"I hope I have not misjudged the situation," she says,

crouching to set the candle on the open floor. Then, like liquid, she moves forward, lifting my chin, and pressing her lips to mine. There is a roaring in my head that is not artillery.

I TURN MY EARS TOWARD THE WINDOW BEFORE I OPEN MY EYES.

It's very quiet and very cold. It is not yet dawn, though the hour is not far.

I reach for her. I want to tell her about my dream, about two wild cats running through the forest steppe. They were free creatures, unhindered by duty or sorrow.

Her skin is like ice.

Her eyes, open, see nothing.

There is movement, a metallic glint and the wire is around my neck before I realize what is happening. Strong hands keep the garrote firm as I claw at my own neck.

"You are a fool," Jean says. "Did you think the KomDiv did not notice your...episodes?"

I kick out, trying to reposition my weight, but he is well grounded. My thrashing only serves to hasten my death.

My heartbeat is pounding in my head. There is a pressure building that blocks out other sounds. My vision darkens and I can't focus. My arms are unusually heavy. And suddenly, I feel calm.

I can see Bobby clearly as she turns her pale face toward me. She blinks, very slowly. The wound across her neck is precise, the blood dark.

"Shift," she says and her voice is not of the living. It scrapes against my bones and burns like a star in my belly.

"Shift," the corpse says, her golden eyes flashing with hellfire. Far away, a large cat growls and there is rage in the sound.

"Shift," she says. "Or die."

With the last of her anger, I plant my bare feet on the wooden floor and push my weight backward, throwing myself against Jean. He is overbalanced and we hit the ground. His hold on my neck tightens.

I toss my head back, catching him, not in the nose as I'd hoped, but against his cheekbone. Something snaps and it is enough.

I scrabble across the floor, gasping. Air, like razors slices into my throat and chest. There is blood in my mouth.

Jean is pushing himself to his feet. His cheek is already purple, his eye closed. He touches the bruise and winces. He sighs deeply.

"If it is not me today," he says, "it will be another tomorrow. You know this is the way."

He is right, of course. I realize I should have suspected something when we were assigned a joint mission. Shifters always work alone. Identities and operations kept secret to protect us or to protect our masters. The radar team has been a final test. And I have failed.

"Come now," he says, leaning down to pull a knife from his boot. He opens his hand and motions for me to approach. "Let's have this done."

I shake my head and step backward. If I can make it to the stair, I might have time to shift before he catches me.

He advances. He can't shift in this space, but with focus, he lends his fierceness to this form. He is ready to kill me.

I stumble on Bobby's shoes, landing hard on my backside amidst our discarded clothing.

Panting, I glare up at him, feeling the rumble of anger in my chest. The growl sets fire to my throat. I grasp my neck, doubling forward and hiding the thing in my hands. The thing I've found under my coat. My whining sounds like wheezing.

He lunges forward, driving his knife down, allowing me no time to retreat.

But I don't need it.

I twist away from him as I bring my own knife up into his chest. He grunts, and then his arms drop to his sides as if he can no longer lift them. His knife lands quietly on top of our clothes. He falls forward, into my hands.

I do my best to lower him to the ground, and there he lays still, trying to draw breath, making strangled, wet noises. His eyes are wide, aware of his death. And he can only watch as I kneel next to him. He slowly shakes his head, setting a powerless hand on my arm. I pull the knife from his chest anyway.

As his body cools, I cover Bobby with my coat. I close her eyes and touch her cheek. May she find the eternal forest steppe.

I dress, and slip out of the window. On the roof, I turn west. I feel the sunrise and, as I make my way across the rooftops, the cold kisses of the first flakes of snow.

Soon, the KomDiv will wake. He will break his fast and he will walk to his office. It is there, I will wait for him. There, I will remind him. The war is over.

SJAN EVARDSSON

Sjan Evardsson has had a long-running love of science fiction and fantasy that began in early childhood and continues to this day. He likes mixing hard sci-fi, cyber-punk, or urban fantasy with human, character-driven narratives.

With five entries, he has placed second in the Life of Writers writing contest three times, and third once. He currently has nearly 30 short stories on Reedsy and is working on making 2021 the year he gets a story published, and the first draft of his novel complete.

Sjan maintains a cover identity as a software engineer in the Pacific Northwest where he lives with his wife and a Norwegian Forest Cat.

Learn more at Evardsson.com

RUNNING AWAY

SJARD EVARDSSON

I t was a mild March morning when Sarah Goode left everything behind. She signed her house and car over to her aunt, a single mother with three children living in a run-down trailer on the reservation. She took a ride share to Reno and bought a one-way ticket on the next bus leaving Nevada. Her mother's last words to her echoed in her mind: "Run away! That's what you always do. It's the only thing you're good at!"

She stepped off the bus the following morning into a damp, misty Seattle. It was no colder than what she was used to, but the moisture crawled under her clothes and wrapped clammy fingers around her narrow shoulders. The mist plastered her straight black hair, tied into two neat braids, around her tawny face. Her eyes flashed obsidian in the grey morning as she scanned for shelter.

There was a large chain coffee shop at her back, but Sarah felt drawn to a smaller shop she could see down the block. A sandwich board sign in front of the shop, protected from the rain by the large awning, read "The Breakfast Stop: Bacon makes everything better! Vegan and Vegetarian items available." Sarah entered the shop and looked around. She didn't feel comfortable tracking in all the water she was currently dripping.

The door opened behind her and a man entered, more soaked than herself. Without saying anything, he pushed past her and walked to the counter, his wet shoes squeaking across the floor. When the women behind the counter treated it as normal, she stepped in further to read the menu. The coffee menu had more items than she had ever heard of, and the breakfast menu was every bit as vast, pulling her into a haze as she tried to make sense of it.

"How can I help you?" the woman behind the cash register asked, jolting Sarah out of her trance.

"I'm sorry," she said, "there's just so much. Can I have a plain coffee with sugar, and do you have some sort of veggie sandwich?" She sat her backpack down and pulled her light jacket off, revealing her slight frame.

"We have meat and egg substitutes," the cashier said, "or would you prefer fresh cooked vegetables?"

"Oh, fresh please," Sarah said, "if that's not too much trouble. For here."

"Not at all. What kind of bread would you like?"

Sarah shrugged. "I don't know, whatever's good."

"Eight dollars even." The cashier pointed at the card reader in front of her and turned to the small kitchen at the back and yelled out, "One garden, house choice!" She poured a cup of drip coffee and placed it in front of Sarah. "Cream and sugar are at the bar over there."

Sarah handed the cashier a ten-dollar bill. "Keep the change."

"Thanks!" The cashier nodded. "You can take a seat and we'll bring it out when it's ready."

Sarah sat at the only unoccupied table, feeling conspicuously out of place. Around her, people were buried in a laptop, tablet, or phone. The few conversations happened over opened devices and were full of tech talk or market speak. It felt more like an open-plan office than a coffee shop.

Sarah watched the woman working in the kitchen. Wavy dark brown hair around a honey-gold face, her features and frame soft, with curves in all the right places. Deep brown hooded eyes, a cute button nose, and teeth that seemed a little too large for her face. It all combined to make her attractive, desirable even. She left the kitchen and walked toward her carrying two small plates in one hand and a take-out cup in the other. "Garden sandwich?"

Sarah blushed at the thought she'd been caught staring. "Uh, y–yes, thank you."

The woman set the sandwich in front of her and took the seat opposite her with her identical sandwich. "I hope it's okay. This is the only place available right now to take my break."

Sarah nodded, trying to get her nerves under control. "Sure, it's your place... I mean your work... I... you know what I mean." She felt the heat crawl up her cheeks and she examined her sandwich to give herself an excuse to look away.

"I get it. So," the woman asked, "just passing through or new to Seattle?"

"Wha–what makes you say that?" Sarah was finding it difficult to speak without her voice cracking.

"You're not dressed for the weather, plus the oversized backpack tells me you came from the bus station." She made a circling gesture with her finger. "Only people who come in here work in the tech offices in the neighborhood or walk down from the bus station."

"I–I'm new here."

"I'm Song. Welcome to Seattle."

"Sorry, I'm Sarah." She took a bite of her sandwich, the mild sourdough perfectly complimenting the roasted portobello and assorted vegetables. "This is really good."

"Thanks," Song said, "I try. I figured I'd have the same. It would be awkward to sit here and eat eggs or meat if you're vegan, and I don't want to scare you off."

"Oh, I'm not like that," Sarah said. "I just can't eat meat; it makes me sick. But I'm okay with other people eating it."

"Good to know. I mostly eat vegetables and eggs, but I occasionally eat meat," Song said.

Sarah looked out the window and scanned the street as far as she could see. "Where could I find a newspaper?" she asked.

"Oh wow." Song tugged at her ear. "You might find some still down on Third Ave, but the machines are usually empty by this time of the morning."

"Crap. I need to find a place to stay, and a job." Sarah sipped at her coffee. "I guess I can stay in a room tonight and start looking tomorrow."

"We're looking for another barista." Song pulled out her phone and handed it to Sarah. "Just point me at your résumé and I'll pass it on to Kate, my boss. That's her at the counter."

Sarah reached into her backpack and pulled out a leather-bound notebook covered in beadwork. She produced a neatly typed résumé and handed it to Song. Amusement played across Song's face.

"Girl, we gotta get you into the twenty-first century." Song laughed. "But that notebook is pretty. Where did you find it?"

"I made it," Sarah said. "I call this pattern washing bear tracks… our word for raccoon means washing bear."

Song smiled. "I love it. And paper works. Is the phone number right?"

"Yes, that's my cell," Sarah said. "So, um, where would I find a room for the night?"

"Well, if you're looking for luxury, just continue on this road towards the big buildings downtown," Song said. "There's a few nice hotels down there. If you're looking on the cheaper side, there's a hostel two blocks south."

"That's probably where I'll go then."

"I should get back to work." Song finished her sandwich and looked at the résumé again. "I'll get this to my boss, but…."

"But?"

"Is it okay if I call you later?" she asked. "Not about the job or anything, but just to talk?"

Sarah tried to stay calm, but ended up blurting out, "I'd love that—er, I'd… um… like that?"

Song winked and left her stunned with her half-finished sandwich and cooling coffee.

SARAH TOOK THE JOB AND SETTLED INTO AN EXTENDED-STAY motel. It was run-down, in a rough neighborhood, with leaky windows, but it was furnished and cheap. Since her workday ended at noon, she began to explore, looking for a wild space she could run. She eventually found a place in Issaquah, a two-hour bus ride away, where she spent every afternoon except Sundays when there weren't enough buses.

She and Song began going out for drinks on Saturdays, which pulled another running day away from her, but she was glad of the company. It had taken the better part of a month to be able to talk to Song without getting tongue-tied. For her part, Song never let a day go by without complimenting Sarah.

The day was busier than usual. One of the tech companies

was having some sort of outdoor festival to raise money for the homeless, and it seemed that most of the Seattle tech sector was in attendance. As it took place on the street outside the Breakfast Stop, they were slammed right up until closing.

"Sarah," Song asked, "are you going to hang out at the festival?"

"No, I've got somewhere I need to be."

"You didn't take a second job, did you?"

"No, I just," Sarah didn't want to say too much, "need to go work out."

"What gym?"

"No, I run… in the forest." As soon as she said it, she felt she might have said too much.

"Oh, cross-country. I used to do that," Song said, "I should get back in the habit. Maybe we could go together some time?"

"Um," Sarah struggled, "yeah, maybe. I need to go."

Sarah hopped on the next bus that would take her down to Second Avenue where she could catch the bus to Issaquah. Something made her uneasy, but she shrugged it off. She concentrated on calming herself on the long ride and wondered how she could ever escalate things with Song. If she knew the truth, she'd leave.

Walking the mile from the stop in Issaquah to the forest, she ran through scenarios in her head. But no matter how she told her, she knew Song would think she was crazy. If she showed her, well, things could go very poorly.

Stepping into the trees she turned off the trail into a small thicket where she removed her clothes and folded them carefully before putting them in her backpack. She covered the pack with branches and let herself transform.

Fingers and toes began to fuse, her face and ears elongating. She dropped to all fours and her limbs thinned and her ribs and pelvis changed shape. Short fur grew over her body and two small horns emerged from her head. When she had finished, she was a pronghorn, known in the Northern Paiute language as tunna.

She ran onto the path and let herself go as fast as she dared in the confining space of the trees. Unlike the plains, where she could run for an hour or more at forty miles an hour, the need to continually change directions limited her to twenty-five or thirty miles an hour. Still, running filled a need deeper than the need for sleep, food, or breathing it seemed.

The brook was her turn-around point. She rested for a moment, drinking the cold, sweet water; her breath making faint vapor in the cool, moist air. Striking at the ground once with her front hoof, she took off to run back to her starting point. She had nearly reached it when the wind shifted, and the scent of danger stopped her in her tracks. In this form, her eyesight made seeing details difficult, but movement was far easier to see. Her hearing and sense of smell were far beyond a human's, and she used all her senses to find the source of the smell.

Movement caught her eye. A small bear: it looked like a black bear, but had a ruff at the collar and a white v-shaped stripe on the chest. The bear stood and raised a paw. That was all she needed. Sarah bolted back the way she had come.

"Sarah! Wait!"

Song's voice made her stop. She turned back, expecting the bear to be closing on her. Instead, Song stood nude in the middle of the trail. Sarah stamped once and tried to act like a wild animal.

"Sarah, I know that's you," Song said. "I'd know your scent anywhere." She held her hand out. "Come here, I'm not going to hurt you."

Sarah stood still as Song approached and stroked her

face. "I'm not going to hurt you." She dropped a half-eaten green pinecone from her hand. "Please, Sarah, it's okay."

With a slight nod, Sarah returned to human form. "Song, are you...?"

Song smiled. "I knew there was something special about you, but I didn't know what."

"So, you're not going to run away?"

"No, I'm not. Are you?"

"Maybe. You scared me."

"I didn't mean to." Song took her hand and started walking back to where she had stashed her clothes. "When you mentioned running in the forest, I realized how much I missed it. I came out here because hardly anyone does. Those that do, I can usually hide from them enough for them to think I'm a young black bear, not an Asiatic bear on the wrong continent."

"I didn't even think about that," Sarah said. "Pronghorns don't live on this side of the mountains, but I need it too much to stop."

"I know." Song followed her into the thicket. "When I came out here, I smelled you." She nodded toward the backpack. Pointing at Sarah's pronghorn tracks, she said, "I also smelled *you*."

Song's clothes were in a plastic bag next to Sarah's backpack. They dressed without speaking.

Sarah turned to Song as she was lacing up her boots. "Now we've seen each other."

Song laughed. "I've been wanting that for a while now, but wasn't sure...."

"How I'd react to you being a bear-woman?"

"No," she said, "whether you were actually interested."

Sarah blushed and turned aside. "You mean that?"

"I've only flirted with you since the first time you stepped into the shop," she said.

Sarah surprised them both by closing the distance and kissing Song. She held the kiss for a few seconds then jumped back. "I—I'm sorry." She ran for the road, putting as much distance between them as she could.

She jumped on the first bus available, which took her to Federal Way instead of Seattle. Sarah spent the time waiting for the next Seattle bus berating herself. *Mother was right. The only thing I'm good at is running away. Idiot!*

The following day, work was strained. Sarah tried her best to avoid Song. She busied herself with cleaning tables, stocking, cleaning the espresso machines, sweeping the floors; anything to avoid the awkward conversation that loomed.

"Sarah, I don't know what you're thinking," Song said, "but it's okay. I'm glad we kissed, but I'd take it back if it meant you'd talk to me again."

Sarah ran into the stock room and began loading her arms with packs of napkins for the tables. Song stepped into the doorway, blocking it.

"Sarah, please, stop running away from me."

Arms laden with bundles of napkins, Sarah turned. "I'm sorry. That's what I do... I run away. It's not your fault."

"You don't have to run anymore. I'll stop chasing. You got ahead of yourself, that's all. When you're ready to talk, you know how to find me." Song placed a gentle hand on her slim shoulder. "That's too many napkins, by the way."

Sarah looked at the bundle she held against her breast like a shield. She nodded and began putting them back on the shelf as Song returned to the kitchen.

Sarah didn't run that afternoon, nor the following. She moved through a haze of confusion. Why was she so unable to be honest with Song, with herself?

Her sleep grew fitful. She remembered the last weeks of

her mother's life. Sarah had one of "the dreams" and her mother didn't want to hear it.

"Mom, please! Stay with me," Sarah said, "and we can go into the city tomorrow."

"Another dream?" Jessie was wearing her lucky casino shirt, ready to drive to Reno for the evening. "You know they don't mean nothing. My mama had those dreams all the time and they was never real."

"Please, don't go. Not tonight."

"I'm going, like it or not," Jessie said. "Now, are you coming with me or not?"

"Mom, it's not safe!"

"Get over it! If you're not going to come, then what am I waiting for? And Ben's boy was hoping to meet you."

"I don't like boys, Mom."

"You've got an evil spirit in you!" Jessie snatched her keys off the table. "Like it or not, you're going to marry a good Paiute boy and have a baby, and she'll be a tunna-woman too."

"I don't have an evil spirit! And I'm not marrying anyone!" Sarah ran out the door towards the fields.

Jessie yelled after her, "Run away! That's what you always do. It's the only thing you're good at!"

That was the last thing Jessie ever said to her daughter. She died at a gas station later that night. She was carjacked and left to bleed out where the assailant shot her by the pumps. It happened exactly the way Sarah had seen in her dream.

IT WAS HALFWAY THROUGH THE WORKDAY WHEN SARAH GOT the courage to send the text that had been sitting as a draft on her phone for the last few days. It said, "Meet me at the running place after work." As soon as she sent it, she felt panic washing over her.

Kate called her into her office. "What's going on?" she asked. "Are you okay? You look like you're on the edge of a panic attack."

Sarah pulled herself together. "It's nothing major. It'll pass. Sorry."

"No," Kate said, "you don't need to apologize for being human. If you need some time off, let me know."

"I'll be okay."

"I don't know what happened between you and Song, but you've both been down in the dumps for the last couple weeks." Kate shook her head. "Maybe I *should* have a no-dating policy in the workplace, but that would be too corporate-evil for words."

"Sorry," Sarah said. "We'll get it figured out this afternoon. That's why I'm on edge."

Kate's eyes softened. "Listen, I don't know you that well, but you seem like a sweet girl. Song is a dear, and she's my friend. I think you two will get along fine once you get past whatever happened last week."

"I hope so."

They closed the shop and Song was waiting for Sarah. She didn't say a word but followed her to the bus stop. They boarded in silence, changed buses in silence, and rode the entire trip sitting next to each other without speaking.

When they got off the bus Song asked, "Are you going to make me wait until we get in the woods to talk?"

Sarah nodded and kept walking. She turned into the thicket she'd come to think of as "hers" on instinct and Song followed her in.

"Are we going to change?" she asked.

"No, just habit," Sarah said. "Walk with me. I'll show you where I run."

They walked for a bit, Sarah looking and listening for anyone else around them. Once she was sure they were alone, she spoke. "I'm sorry. Things got too intense and I freaked out. I run. The last thing my mother said to me was that running away was the only thing I was good at."

"Is that why you came to Seattle?" Song asked. "To run away from something?"

Sarah nodded. "I'm expected to marry a 'good Paiute boy' and have a daughter to carry on the tunna-woman tradition. I'm supposed to bless new babies, and weddings, and crap like that. But the dreams…"

"My mother ran away most of her life," Song said. "There are hunters of bear-people in China. They say they have amulets that force them to change, and then kill them for their pelt, which is supposed to have magical properties or something."

"What good does that do?" Sarah asked. "Once you sleep, or go unconscious, or die, like my great-grandmother did, you change back."

"That's what the amulet is supposed to prevent." Song shrugged. "I think it's bullshit, but I do believe my mother was being hunted. So that's what she ran away from. What about you?"

"I'd like to say it was the pressure and expectations, but really, it's the dreams." Sarah grabbed hold of her courage and carried on. "I dream of people's deaths. Not natural deaths; violent deaths, accidental deaths."

"Wow, just anyone?"

"Only people I'm close to." Tears pooled in Sarah's eyes. "My mother didn't believe the dreams. My grandmother had them too. I told her not to go to Reno, but she went." Sarah sniffed and took a deep breath. "I'm sorry, I didn't mean to dump all that on you."

Song put her arm around Sarah and pulled her close.

"You can dump your troubles on me at any time. And if you have a dream about me, I'll do whatever you say."

"You promise?"

"I promise." Song stopped and pulled Sarah around to face her. "If it's okay with you, I'm going to kiss you now."

Sarah nodded and let herself be carried away by the kiss.

THAT NIGHT, THE DREAM WAS BACK, BUT THIS TIME IT changed. Her mother turned into Song, the carjacker split into two Asian men in suits, and the gas station morphed into the Breakfast Spot. The two men pulled out pistols and forced Song into a black van.

In the dream, she followed the van, able to see inside. Song was locked in a cage, and one of them tied a band with a charm around her wrist. As soon as the band was tied, Song transformed, unable to prevent it. Her bear form shredded her clothes and swiped at the bars to no effect.

The van pulled into a warehouse with a green and yellow door and the cage was unloaded. One of the men placed a rifle at the base of her skull and pulled the trigger. Sarah jolted awake.

She grabbed her phone and called Song, but there was no answer. "Song, when you get this message call me right back. Whatever you do today, *do not go to work!*"

Sarah dressed as quickly as she could and called a ride-share to get her to work. She was an hour early and no one was there yet. She tried calling Song again and thought she heard her phone's K-Pop ringtone inside the cafe. Unsure whether what she had heard was real, she dialed again as she allowed her ears to transform. Song's phone was somewhere inside, but Song wasn't.

Desperate, Sarah called Kate. "Hi, it's Sarah, I'm sorry for bothering you this early, but I'm trying to reach Song. It's an emergency."

"Are you going to be out today?"

"N—no, I'm actually already here. I tried calling Song, but her phone's inside."

"You look like you saw a ghost. What happened?" Kate's voice was coming from the phone and from beside her.

Sarah swirled around startled, her eyes changing for a split-second. She ended the call and tried to smooth her hair. "What time does she usually come in?"

"She's always here before you, but only because her bus shows up five minutes before yours," Kate said. "You said her phone was here?"

"Yeah, I tried calling, but I heard it ringing in there."

Kate unlocked the door and turned off the alarms. "I have to do the books. Why don't you come to the office and tell me what's going on?" She dialed Song from her phone and K-Pop echoed from the kitchen. "How can she go all night without her phone?"

Sarah wanted to run, to ignore the dream, to say nothing. Kate would ridicule her, call her delusional, maybe have her committed. The sight of the rifle against Song's skull flashed in her mind.

"You look like you're going to run away," Kate said. "I'm not going to say anything. Just tell me what's wrong."

Sarah told her about the dream. Then she told her about the dream about her mother, and how that ended. She explained how she had dreamt her death in vivid detail, how her mother tried to convince her it was nothing. She told her of her mother's constant argument that her dreams about the deaths of others on the reservation were not real, even though those who ignored her warnings died exactly as she had seen.

Kate nodded as she listened. The books lay open next to

her, but she was ignoring them. When Sarah had finished, Kate turned to her and grabbed her hands. "My aunt had the sight. She ended up in a hospital."

"I'm not crazy," Sarah said.

"I didn't say you were. Neither was my aunt." Kate opened her phone and copied Song's address down on a sticky-note. "You're worried about her," she said, "and based on your history, that's for good reason. Take her phone with you and make sure she's okay. She doesn't need to come in today."

"Thank you." Sarah left the office and picked up Song's phone from the kitchen. The van was parked in front of the cafe, and the bus was just pulling away. Sarah screamed at the top of her lungs, "RUN, SONG!"

Kate bolted out of her office just in time to see Song abducted by the two gunmen and bundled into the van. She dialed 911 without hesitation while Sarah ran towards the van. "Sarah, no! They have guns!"

The van pulled away before Sarah could reach the front door. Her only hope was to be at the warehouse before them. The dream replayed in her mind. She knew where the warehouse was. Sarah began stripping as fast as she could. "This is going to seem really weird, but I'm going to need you to open the door for me in a minute."

"What are you do—what *are* you?" Kate stared as Sarah transformed into a pronghorn. She stood transfixed, mouth agape.

Sarah stamped her hoof at her and gestured toward the door with her head. All her muscles quivered with bundled energy, adrenaline pumping her up. When Kate failed to move, Sarah went to the door and attempted to open it with her hooves, having no effect other than banging on the door.

Shaken out of her trance, Kate opened the door for her, and Sarah bolted out into the street.

Following the dream, Sarah retraced the path of the van.

She knew it was probably on Second Avenue by now, but she could run against traffic on Third and get ahead of them. The asphalt and concrete hurt her hooves, but she ignored it and ran on.

Worried that she might get lost if she stayed off the path from the dream for too long, she turned downhill and ran down to Second Avenue. It was easier to maneuver around the traffic going in the same direction. She guessed she was going about thirty-five to forty miles an hour. Her hooves ached from the road and sidewalks, but she focused on her breath. Deep, full breaths that made the pace suitable for endurance.

Sarah crossed an intersection and stopped. This was wrong, it wasn't the right way. She circled back and scanned the buildings. *That way.* She took off on her new trajectory. Before long, she saw the warehouses. Rows and rows of identical warehouses, but all she needed to do was find the one door. Green and yellow. But in her current state, colors were unidentifiable.

She looked up and down the street, looking for movement. Satisfied that she was alone, she transformed. While a wild animal running through the city gets attention, so does a naked woman in the warehouse district, although of a very different kind. The door she was looking for was two buildings ahead. Her feet and hands ached from running on the hard roads, but she'd been ignoring it long enough that she barely noticed how much running as a barefoot person hurt.

The large cargo door was closed, and not something she could open. She tried the smaller office door to one side, but it was locked tight. She wandered around the warehouse and found a low window. With a piece of two-by-four from the pile of smashed pallets she broke the window and did her best to get all the glass out of the frame.

Sarah dropped a piece of cardboard in to protect her feet from the glass and crawled through the window to a darkened room. Giving her eyes a minute to adjust, she could make out the room. A small bathroom with one large handicap stall, in which she stood, and a sink. She stepped out of the stall and the lights flickered on. Motion detector.

The door to the bathroom was open to the warehouse beyond. She moved into the space cautiously, brandishing the two-by-four. It wouldn't be enough of a weapon against their guns. She wandered through the warehouse looking for something better. A crowbar would be nice, but slow to swing. A baseball bat would be fast and dangerous. If only she had a gun. There was nothing in the warehouse that she could use.

What am I looking for? My horns are small, but they're sharp and so are my hooves. She dropped the two-by-four and sat behind one of the rows of shelves. When she heard the overhead door opening, she transformed, waiting for the van to stop. Once she heard the van shut off, she ran out to stand directly in front of it. She could hear Song growling from within the van.

The men jumped out, yelling what she guessed was Chinese. One of them pulled his pistol and she ran for the shelves. Having already seen the layout she knew where she had to turn and where she could run. She kicked at the shelves as she ran past, hoping to make enough noise to get them to follow.

One followed her, the other running down the next row over. She ran to the end of the row then turned left, passing the row the other man was running in. Once out of his sight, she stopped and turned, waiting for him to turn the corner. As he did, she reared up and slashed at him with her hooves before turning to run again.

The commotion behind her told her this was her chance.

She ran for the van, shifting as she neared to open the rear door. Song was in a panic, trying to break out of the cage. Sarah opened the latch and Song pushed her out of the way running out. She recovered and stepped out of the van and shifted again.

The man she'd attacked had blood pouring down his face from a gash on his forehead. Song was nowhere to be seen, and with the yelling the two men were doing, she couldn't hear her. Movement to her left caught her attention; Song was circling behind them.

Sarah charged the uninjured man, barreling into him at full speed. Her small horns pierced flesh and crashed into his pelvis. It felt like running into a wall, but it was enough to put him on his back. She stomped on the hand still holding the pistol until he dropped it. Once it was free, she kicked it out of his reach.

She jumped away and transformed to pick up the pistol. She'd never pointed a gun at anything other than a target before, but she didn't hesitate. "Song, disarm the other one."

"Another one?" the man she had at gunpoint on the floor asked. "Where did you come from?"

"Shut up! On your face, spread your arms and legs, and lay there." She checked the magazine and made sure there was a round in the chamber. "You move and I find out how good a Glock shoots."

Song let out a long growl. She sat on the chest of the other man who had given up. Without taking her eyes off the man she was pointing the pistol at, Sarah moved to her side. "They tied something around your wrist so you can't transform, right?"

Song nodded emphatically and let out a low growl.

"Here's how this is going to work." Sarah kicked the man Song sat on. "You remove the band, or I shoot your friend...and Song rips out your throat."

"He doesn't speak English," the other man said.

"Then you better translate, and don't get cute. My mother always said I had an evil spirit, and I might just prove it."

He said something in Chinese and the other man answered in panicked tones. "He says he'll do it. Please don't kill us."

He motioned to his side pocket. Sarah checked it and pulled out the knife that was there. She opened it and handed it to him. "One scratch on her, you both die."

The other man translated for him. He nodded and felt along Song's wrist. On finding the band, he slid the knife blade beneath and cut it loose.

Song transformed and rolled off him. She coughed and moaned. "Fuck! My head."

"Are you okay, Song?"

"What the fuck? My head feels like it's going to explode."

"Get his gun."

Song patted the man down. "He doesn't have one."

"Okay, on your face like your partner!"

When he didn't move, Sarah pointed the pistol at him. "I'm going to shoot your friend if he doesn't get on his face now!"

The other man translated, and he slowly rolled over, getting into the same position. Song patted along his back, found a pistol there, and took it. "Do you have a phone?" she asked.

"Kind of hard to carry one like this." Sarah nodded toward the other man. "Keep an eye on them. I'm going to check him out."

Song nodded. She stood with one foot on the man's ankle. "You move, you die."

Sarah checked the man's pockets. "No phones. I'll check the van. You good to watch them for now?"

"I got it."

There were no phones in the van, but it did have an emergency roadside assistance button. She pushed it and a woman's voice came on, "Tristar assistance, what is your emergency?"

"There are two men here with guns," she said. "They kidnapped us and stripped us, and they're holding us in a warehouse. Send help, please."

"Police are being dispatched to your location now. Is anyone in need of medical attention?"

"One of the men, probably. They started fighting and that's how we got loose."

Sirens began nearing. It sounded like every police car in the city was on their way to the warehouse.

Sarah left the van, the Tristar woman still talking. She got close to Song and whispered, "They snatched you at the breakfast spot, and me a block down when I was running after them. They threw my clothes out on the trip and then started on yours. When we got to the warehouse, they argued and fought, and that's how we got loose and grabbed a pistol that one of them dropped."

Song whispered back, "Got it."

"Kate, um…knows what I am." Sarah said.

"You told her?" Song's eyes were wide.

"No," she said, "I had to change to come rescue you."

AT THE POLICE STATION, SARAH CALLED KATE TO LET HER know what was going on. "Could you bring my bag with my change of clothes, and see if Song has her running clothes in the locker? After those guys snatched us, they threw my clothes out and shredded Song's."

"After they snatched *you*?" Kate asked.

"Yeah, you were right, I shouldn't have run after them, but if I hadn't…" she said.

"I'll bring your stuff and see what I can find for Song," Kate said, "and both of your phones. I've been charging hers. I told the police that you ran after the van, but not about the stuff that would make me seem crazy."

"Thanks," Sarah said, her voice dropping to almost a whisper. "Sorry for messing up your day."

"No. You're *not* the one that needs to apologize. Neither of you," she said. "Did you at least hurt them a little bit? Turn into a lion and slash them or something?"

"It doesn't work like that," Sarah said. "If you really want to know more, we can talk about it some other time."

After the longest two hours of her life, Sarah was finally free to go, but Song was still talking to the detectives. Sarah looked at the door, and then back to the desk where Song was talking with the officer. As much as she wanted to flee, she sat down to wait for Song instead.

When she had finally finished, Song offered her hand to Sarah. "Thank you for not running away," she said.

Sarah took her hand and rose, giving her a small kiss. "Thank you for giving me a reason to stay."

JO NIEDERHOFF

Jo Niederhoff has never met a bear she doesn't like. It also took her until she was fifteen to meet a story she didn't like. Luckily, those stories are few and far between, though it's hard to say whether she's lucky or just not picky.

Most of what she reads is fantasy and science fiction, though she has been trying to branch out into more niche subjects, like slice of life.

She can be found on the outskirts of Denver, Colorado, where she spends her time writing, acting in community theater productions, and wrangling small children, most of whom seem like they belong in a story of their own.

Learn more at Twitter.com/JoNiederhoff

GRACE FROM THE STRONG
JO NIEDERHOFF

Sigrid was lucky. They'd let her live.

She hadn't thought it was lucky at the time, though. Not with the binding runes still prickling on the back of her neck and the lingering sense that her body was not entirely her own. (Or perhaps that it was too entirely her own. The sensation was too new for her to tell.) She hadn't wanted to die, of course, but she hadn't thought there was anything particularly lucky in her situation.

She'd been caught with one of Mistress Landvik's silver rings. Other stories had come out, about Sigrid Nilsdotter. Things tended to go missing from the houses she worked at. Small things. Valuable things. Those eagle eyes that could pick out any spot of dirt needing to be cleaned had turned her into a thieving magpie.

She'd stolen enough and so often that no one wanted to consider it her first offense, even though it was the first time she'd been brought before the magistrate. No one spoke out on her behalf. She'd thought at least one person would, but even Kari held her tongue.

Faithless Kari. Sigrid wished she could turn in her seat and glare at her, but she didn't dare move. She'd already been paraded before everyone as a thief and locked up. She didn't want to find out what more they could do to her before passing sentence. Things were already bad enough.

Not that it would matter in the end. She would be hanged. Whatever happened before then couldn't possibly be worse, except for the runes. They had burned as they were etched into the back of her neck, and she had felt her skin prickling as it healed over them. She still felt the prickling now, though it was faint; a phantom of the pain she had felt before.

She'd shifted in her seat, waiting. She would be hanged. She knew it. Everyone knew it. All they waited for was to know the date.

But then the magistrate pronounced her banished instead. Sigrid blinked several times, not sure whether she was blinking away tears or shock. She knew she was lucky. She wasn't going to die, at least not immediately. Banishment gave her a chance at survival.

But her wings had been clipped. She could still feel the lack of them in her mind and every part of her body. She was stuck in her human body, stumbling along on clumsy feet, having to remind herself every few seconds that she couldn't just take to the sky and fly away. She would have to walk.

She left Sogndal on foot, following the road north and away. It wasn't long before her feet began to ache and her legs to cramp. She had never walked so long in her life. It was a different sort of weariness from a long day of cleaning and serving. Then her whole body moved. Now it was just her legs and feet, though she could feel it in her back as well as the day wore on.

And she could not fly. That felt like the greatest punishment of all.

Sigrid moved away from the road late in the afternoon. She didn't want to be found by anyone, alone and vulnerable as she was.

Safety was relative. There would be fewer people in the mountains, but they would be hardier there, more ruthless. They would be what she had to become.

And there was more in the mountains than just men.

It was light enough for her to find some berries for her dinner. They didn't do much to fill her stomach, but they were better than nothing. She wasn't starving yet. She had felt that sort of hunger before and would know when she was in danger.

Her stomach was already complaining. She curled tighter around herself.

She wanted a full meal. She wanted a warm bed.

She wanted to go home.

She couldn't have any of those things. It was pointless to wish for what couldn't be. Closing her eyes against the evening sunlight, she let herself drift into sleep.

WHEN SIGRID WOKE, THE SUN HAD RISEN. THE MIST MADE everything dim and grey, and it was hard to make out anything around her, especially with her weak human eyes. If she could have become a bird, even for a moment…

But she knew she couldn't. It would only hurt her more to wish for what she couldn't have. She would have to push those thoughts away.

Even without being able to see through the mist, she knew something was watching her.

Sigrid lay still, every muscle in her body tense. The binding runes strained against the urge to flee, to let her bones shift in her body and feathers sprout from her skin.

The prickling all through her body reminded her that she couldn't escape that easily. If she ran, she would have only her ungainly human legs. Whoever was watching her could catch her if they wanted to. She had never before realized how fragile a human body could be. She had no talons now. There were only her ragged little nails and pitiful teeth.

Whoever watched her could catch her if she stayed still, too. She wished she had a knife, but even a rock would be better than the nothing she had now. With a rock she could strike someone. It didn't matter whether it had a sharp edge or was blunt. All it needed was weight.

Whoever was watching her already knew she was here. They might as well know that she knew the same.

Trembling, Sigrid sat up. "Hello?" she whispered. "Who's there?" Her voice sounded thin and faint in the early morning air.

At first, there was no answer. The silence felt worse than whatever was out there, until she heard rustling in the distance. That was worse than the silence had been. Sigrid leaned forward, eyes wide, trying to see through the mist.

She saw nothing more than a dark, bulky shape moving heavily through the darkness. As it grew closer, Sigrid drew back until her back pressed against a tree and she could go no further.

A huge brown bear emerged from the trees. This was how she would die, then, less than a full day after leaving Sogndal. She would be torn apart and eaten, and no one would ever know. Her bones would be scattered about, and she would just be another banished thief.

It was already too late to run. It had been too late from the first moment the bear saw her.

Sigrid closed her eyes, bracing herself. No one would know how she died, or how she acted just before her death.

Still, she couldn't bring herself to wail and sob, or go to pieces completely. Something in her rebelled against the notion. She would be strong, for as long as she could, even if the only one to know would be her.

Seconds passed. Sigrid couldn't say how many. All she could count was the beating of her heart, and that raced faster than she could keep track of. The sound pounded through her body, echoing in her ears, only drowned out by her ragged, uneven breathing.

Had it been five minutes? Six? She couldn't be certain. The bear should have eaten her by now, though. She ought to be devoured. Sigrid cracked open one eye.

No one else was about… The bear had gone, without a sound, and she was alone with the trees and the slope of the mountain. As minutes passed and her heartbeat slowed, she began to hope the bear really had gone. Bears were not crafty creatures. This one must have lost interest in her and wandered off. It was time for her to move on, too. Muscle by muscle, Sigrid's body relaxed, and she stretched her limbs.

Her foot brushed against something warm and feathered, and she looked down. A ptarmigan lay before her, its body pierced by large teeth. It hadn't been devoured; if anything, it looked as though it had been carried as gently as a great beast could manage.

Hunger overcame all else, even curiosity. Sigrid wrenched the feathers off the ptarmigan, scattering them about her like brown snow. She had no fire, nor any way to make one, so she dug her teeth into the skin, tearing it open. Hot blood spilled onto her hands and over her tongue. She knew the taste; she had fed on blood often as a bird of prey. This was no different.

So she told herself. She would tell herself anything to keep from vomiting.

She ate as much of the ptarmigan as she could, ripping the slick, gamy meat with her teeth. She swallowed the slippery organs whole and licked the bones clean. Her stomach felt heavy and her hands were bloody, but she was full now in a way she hadn't been since being dragged from Mistress Landvik's.

Full of ptarmigan, Sigrid went back to the berry bush and ate a few to slake her thirst. Berries wouldn't content her forever, though. Sooner or later, she would have to find a stream.

The day proved to be a bright one, and Sigrid set about exploring the mountain. The air had the cool of late summer, but by noon, she was already thirsty. For now, it was only a dry throat, but she knew the signs of thirst well enough to be frightened, and the chattering of a stream almost made her weep with relief. If she was lucky, it would be large enough to have fish, so she could ease her hunger as well as her thirst. Her stomach already clamored for more.

Sigrid froze as soon as she reached the stream. It was beautiful, water glinting in the sun, and it looked more than large enough to host fish.

But sitting just on the other bank was a bear.

She couldn't say whether it was *the* bear. This bear was large and brown, just as the other had been, but it looked so much like any other bear that she couldn't be certain.

She stared at the bear, and the bear stared back. It leaned forward, snuffling. As it rose onto its four paws, Sigrid took a step back, then another. She would be ready this time. The bear could outrun her, but there were trees all about, and she was light enough to climb above the bear's reach. She could only hope the tree would be sturdy enough to withstand the bear's weight slamming against it.

The bear's front paws splashed into the stream, and Sigrid fled. At the first tree she found with a low branch, she jumped and scrambled up, tearing her palms and skirt against the rough bark. There was another within reach, and another just above that. Her arms burned with the strain of pulling up her body, but she couldn't stop, not until she was above the bear's reach.

When the branch beneath her shook from her weight, she stopped and glanced down. The bear had followed her. It stood on four feet at the base of the tree, staring up at her with its dark eyes.

Sigrid trembled. "What do you want?" she cried, hardly caring that it couldn't understand her. "Why are you still after me?"

The bear said nothing. It didn't so much as growl. It merely stepped back, revealing a fish lying on the ground. Even from so high, Sigrid could see that it had the same marks that had been on the ptarmigan. It had been carried as gently as a bear could manage, and it was meant for her.

Her stomach growled. Even a raw fish was appealing.

Was this the same bear? Why would it want to feed her?

What did it want?

Sigrid slowly descended the tree, not taking her eyes off the bear as she searched with her feet for the next branch. It had moved further back, but it still felt too close for comfort.

It didn't charge forward. Even when Sigrid paused on the lowest branch, where it could have reached her on its hind legs, it didn't move. It stayed perfectly still, watching her, waiting for… something. What, she didn't know

In the end, she had to act. The bear wasn't moving, but she would. She breathed in, breathed out, and jumped down to the ground.

The bear did nothing.

As quickly as she could, Sigrid grabbed the fish, stuffed it into the bodice of her dress, and pulled herself back up into the tree. She didn't climb so far this time and looked down sooner.

The bear was exactly where it had been before. As far as she could tell, it hadn't moved at all, not even to wiggle a paw.

The fish was messier than the ptarmigan had been, and harder to eat, especially perched above the ground. By the time she finished, her hands and dress were filthy, and she didn't want to imagine what her mouth looked like.

She licked her lips. Now that she was sated, the lingering taste wasn't nearly as appealing.

The bear was still there, of course. It hadn't even taken its gaze off her. When it saw she had finished, it rose and walked a few steps toward the tree. Halfway to the base of the trunk it paused and looked up at her. Then it turned and began to lumber away.

It didn't lumber far. It stopped again by a nearby spruce and looked over its shoulder as though it was waiting for her.

That was ridiculous. Everything about this was ridiculous.

Sigrid lowered herself onto the next branch. Her hands were slippery against the bark, and she stopped, trembling.

The bear was still waiting.

"What do you want?" Sigrid called. "Do you want me to come with you?"

The bear nodded.

It was strange to see. The great head descended slowly, almost majestically, and for a moment, it was impossible for Sigrid to believe this creature would devour her messily. It seemed far too dignified for that.

She lowered herself to the next branch. "Are you going to eat me?"

The bear shook its head.

"Do you promise?"

Another nod.

If there was any expression on its face, she couldn't make it out. It was just a bear, looking at her, promising not to eat her.

Sigrid lowered herself to the ground. The dirt and grass felt solid beneath her feet, just as the tree felt solid against her hand. Every bit of it was real.

She took a few steps forward. Once the bear saw that she was willing to follow, it lumbered off through the trees. If there was any time to turn and run, it was now. If she was swift and silent, the bear might not even notice until she was well away.

But she followed. She didn't feel as though she had any other choice. The bear was trusting her, ridiculous as it sounded, and it was probably unwise to betray a bear's trust.

THEY WENT NORTH FOR MILES, UNTIL SIGRID'S LEGS BURNED and her feet ached. *One more step*, she told herself. *One more step, and then I can collapse.*

One step became two, then, three, then four, but she wouldn't let herself reach five. If she had only taken one step, she wouldn't feel how far she had walked.

She must have taken one step a thousand times or more before the bear stopped and turned. She was too tired to feel anything but the shadow of fear. Would the bear eat her here? It looked no different from anywhere else in the mountains, but there might be some difference for the bear. It might be sacred somehow.

If it was, Sigrid couldn't tell. The trees rose from the earth just the same, and the slope of that earth rose toward the sky as it did everywhere else. It was a mountain, like any other mountain.

The bear approached her, snuffling. It only reached her breast on all fours, but it was far too large to be so close to her. It sniffed at her, walking around in a circle. Sigrid stood frozen, heart pounding, eyes wide until the bear turned away to move further up the mountain.

She couldn't. She simply couldn't. She didn't even try to keep her legs under her but crumpled to the ground, catching herself on her hands. Then her arms gave way, and she lay on the earth, breathing hard, eyes closed.

She could sleep here. It would be so easy just to let herself drift off. She felt no fear of the future. She felt hardly anything at all.

Then the bear nudged her.

It was a gentle nudge, but that was still enough for Sigrid to open her eyes and look blearily up at the bear.

"I can't," she whispered. "I can't get up again. Please don't make me."

The bear huffed, then lowered slowly to its knees. It took Sigrid a long moment to realize what it wanted.

She licked her cracked lips. "Are you sure?" she whispered.

The bear bowed its head, solemn and grave. For just a moment, Sigrid felt -- she couldn't say exactly what she felt. It was like something swelling up within her body, expanding like a boil but without the threat of festering. Whatever she felt, it was clean.

She would try. She had enough strength for that.

It was a near thing. By the time she'd climbed atop the bear, she lacked the strength to sit up. All she could do was lie on her stomach; fingers tangled in the fur. "Thank you," she murmured. If the bear heard, it didn't react.

They walked on for some minutes longer before the bear rocked, shaking Sigrid loose onto a pile of grass and leaves. It was soft beneath her body and smelled green and damp and rotting.

It didn't matter. It was the most comfortable thing she'd had to lie on in days.

For a while, she lay still, staring at the bear but seeing nothing. One of her hands was outstretched, and as the bear walked back and forth, it stepped over her arm carefully. Every one of its steps was careful near her, she realized.

It was a good thing, too. If it stepped on her, it would probably crush her.

Sigrid smiled faintly. It felt strange to have someone looking after her, enough that the bear was not the strangest part.

It was dark when Sigrid opened her eyes. A little starlight came through the tops of the trees, but only enough for her to see shadows and shapes. If there was a moon, she couldn't see it. All she saw were the stars and the woman beside her.

Sigrid blinked slowly, lazily. She couldn't see much of the woman. She was tall, with long hair, and her face was pointed up toward the stars. She was looking for something, but what it was, Sigrid couldn't tell.

Time didn't seem to pass in the darkness. She knew the stars must be moving across the sky, but for that moment, everything seemed still.

Then the woman turned to look at her. Her face was shrouded in shadow, but Sigrid could still feel her gaze. Her lips parted to speak, but nothing came out.

SHE WOKE TO BRILLIANT MORNING LIGHT THAT MADE HER blink and shade her eyes. She was alone and thought the bear must have abandoned her until she saw a hare lying on the ground beside a sharp stone.

She would have been happy for fire as well, but the stone was better than nothing, and she set to work skinning the rabbit.

By the time it was cleaned and devoured, the bear had returned. Sigrid wiped her mouth and hands on her skirt, though she knew it wouldn't do much good. She still looked filthy, and now her clothes must look even worse than before, if that was at all possible.

"Is there a stream nearby?" she asked. "I need something to drink."

The bear nodded and walked away, leaving Sigrid to scramble to her feet and follow after. At least the bear was moving slowly, so it didn't take her long to catch up.

"I had a dream last night," she said into the silence. The bear glanced at her out of the corner of its eye. "It was very strange. I lay in the forest, as I had been when you dropped me, and it was very late. I could see the stars through the branches of the trees, but the moon wasn't there. I saw a woman, too. She sat right next to me, looking up at the stars, and then she looked at me."

If there had been more to the dream, she couldn't remember it now.

"It was very strange," she said again.

The bear made no response.

"Do bears dream? I never had a reason to think about it before."

The bear didn't answer, through sound or sign. Perhaps there was no reason to. They had reached the stream by now, and Sigrid hurried forward, dropping to her knees to wash her hands and face in the frigid water.

The cold was refreshing, and she felt more alert than she had in days.

The bear was beside her, a little upstream, dipping its snout into the water to drink. After watching it for a moment, Sigrid stepped over the stream and skirted around it so she could be upstream and drink water that hadn't just passed through a bear's mouth.

For a while, they drank in companionable silence. When Sigrid finished, she sat back on the ground, stretching out her legs and staring up at the sky. She had noticed earlier how bright it was, but now she saw that it was a brilliant blue, the same color as Kari's eyes.

Kari's eyes that had watched her as she was banished. Kari's eyes that had likely not shed a single tear on learning she was gone. Sigrid had thought she was being careful with Kari, that someone so soft-spoken would surely feel more for her than she ever could. Instead, here she was pining, while Kari likely carried on with her life. She probably hadn't thought about her at all.

When the bear finished drinking, Sigrid sat up again and dried her hands on her skirt. "How long will you let me stay with you?" she asked. "I'm glad you saved my life, but you probably don't want me following you around. You can send me away whenever you want. Just…just please don't eat me."

She hadn't meant for her voice to crack that way. She hadn't meant to sound so weak.

The bear looked up at her. It said nothing.

That didn't surprise her. She would have been surprised if it had spoken, or given her any answer beyond yes or no. She would have been surprised if the bear had done anything at all but look at her.

The bear stepped across the stream and stood on the bank beside her. For a moment they only looked at each other, and then the bear walked away.

Sigrid followed.

The day was more peaceful than she would have expected in the wilderness. Sometimes she heard a bird calling out, but beyond that, they might have been the only two creatures alive.

There was something wonderful about being out so far from everyone she'd ever known, and with a bear by her side, no one would dare come near her. Why should she worry about Kari? She had the company of a far better friend, and one who she hoped would prove more loyal.

"Do you do this often?" she asked. "Have you found other wanderers before and helped them survive?"

The bear shook its head.

"So, I'm the first?"

It nodded.

"Why me?"

There was no answer. The bear didn't even nod. It simply kept walking, and Sigrid walked with it.

"Is there something special about me?"

Again, there was no answer. Sigrid tried not to let the silence infect the air around her, but all at once, everything had grown unsettling and strange. Even the mountains, which she had almost begun to trust, seemed to bristle with menace.

The bear still hadn't looked at her. Sigrid decided to dare for one more question.

"How long will you keep me?"

Again, there was no answer. That time, she hadn't really expected one.

THEY SOON FELL INTO A FAMILIAR PATTERN. THEY WOULD walk a while, then rest. The bear would get food for Sigrid, then for itself. They never wandered far from the stream, so Sigrid was always able to wash the worst of the blood off herself and drink something fresh and cold.

The water chilled her from the inside. It felt bright and wild, like drinking a winter breeze. Sigrid felt bright and wild when she raised her head to see the bear just a bit away from her.

She shouldn't grow used to this. It was dangerous. It could kill her.

It couldn't kill her worse than being hanged. She supposed that was some consolation.

Sometimes she woke in the middle of the night and saw the woman. Most of the time, the woman was awake, staring up at the stars. Those nights, Sigrid lay perfectly still, breathing slowly, watching through half-lidded eyes. She never once saw the woman's face, but the shape of her body was enough to know that she was real.

Then one night, she caught her sleeping.

Summer had waned, and the nights grew colder. Sigrid had lain closer to the bear than before, thinking nothing of it until she was already half asleep. When she woke, she expected to feel the bear beside her, but it wasn't. Instead, she saw the woman.

For several breaths, Sigrid lay still, watching to see whether the woman was really asleep... When it was practically impossible for her to lie still any longer, she shifted onto her side, propping herself up on her elbow.

The moon wasn't quite full, but it was bright, and Sigrid could see more of the woman than she had before.

She was broad, as though she had done a great deal of work in her life, or perhaps as though she had been born to work. Her face was broad as well, and a tangled dark mass of hair surrounded it. One of her bare feet stuck out into the moonlight, and Sigrid saw that it was callused and rough, more so than even her own.

The woman was wrapped in a bearskin. Sigrid felt as though she should have noticed that before. She felt as though it should have been the very first thing she noticed.

It was a long time before she could fall asleep again. Until then, she lay awake, blinking in the darkness, always imagining that the sun was just at the horizon.

THE BEAR ATE A GREAT DEAL MORE NOW. SIGRID DID AS WELL, feasting on the bear's leavings. She'd grown used to eating raw meat, and perhaps it helped that she had eaten it as a bird before. It wasn't entirely foreign to her body. It was just foreign to *this* body.

This body still felt strange to her sometimes. She still felt the urge to leap up into the sky and take flight. She'd grown used to being trapped on the ground, but her old habits were as much a part of her body as her muscles and blood. They couldn't be forced out of her so easily.

A bird would have had feathers to keep itself warm. It grew colder by the day, and Sigrid often found herself shivering when she woke in the morning. The bear lay beside her, but she never felt entirely warm enough. It was as though the warmth had been taken away from her partway through the night and only returned with the dawn.

Even with the sun setting sooner each day, they stopped for the night before it fully set. The bear seemed eager to sleep, and Sigrid couldn't blame it.

Her. She couldn't blame her.

One cloudy day, as it grew dark well before Sigrid felt it should have, she settled herself on a mound of dried leaves, trying to ignore how they pricked her skin. The bear snuffled about, as though testing the ground, before settling beneath a tree. After a few moments of silence, Sigrid gathered up an armful of her leaves and moved next to the bear.

"You can't leave me now," she said. "I'll freeze without you." She'd meant to say the words lightly, the way she said so much, but she realized as she lay down beside the slowly heaving belly, they were deadly earnest.

Slowly, Sigrid reached out a hand and laid it on the bear's side. She hadn't reached out to touch her before, but now it felt easy, almost effortless. The bear was warm, steady, comforting. As night settled in, Sigrid felt as though they were the only two living things in the world.

"Will you let me stay with you in winter?" she asked. "Wherever you go, can I go with you?"

The bear growled, but it wasn't an angry sound. It only sounded irritated, as though Sigrid had woken her from a pleasant sleep.

She smiled to herself, closing her eyes. This was more than just pleasant. It was companionable. She hadn't had that sort of feeling in years.

She didn't think she'd ever had it.

"I want to stay with you," she said. "I don't want to be tossed aside, especially not in winter. I don't know how it's begun, but I've grown fond of you. I know it sounds impossible--a woman fond of a bear--but it's true. I want to stay near you. I...I like you."

She could have said love. She was tempted to. Instead, she lifted herself just a little and rested her head on the bear's belly. At once, she was surrounded by the smell of fur and life. It was a scent she'd been growing steadily more used to, but it struck her differently now that she had the bear for a pillow. It was like being embraced.

She couldn't possibly give this up. She couldn't ever be asked to.

"Please," she said. "Let me stay with you."

The bear made a sound that was a bit like a grumble, but if so, it was a pleased grumble. Sigrid could hear the difference, and she couldn't help smiling. If her arms would have fit, she would have thrown them around the bear, squeezing as tightly as she dared.

Then the sun set.

Sigrid only understood that was what happened later. In that moment, all she knew was that something was happening to the bear. Her body tensed all over, and Sigrid flinched, not knowing whether she should draw back or hold on all the tighter. She compromised by doing nothing at all.

The bear twisted against her, and her body drew in against itself, as though she was vanishing. Sigrid tightened her grip, pulling herself up to hold onto the bear. "It's all right," she gasped. "It's all right, I'm here. I'm here."

The bear made no sound at all. She only continued to shrink, as though something inside her was pulling her away. Sigrid bit her lip, trying not to imagine what was happening. It wasn't easy; she kept thinking of everything inside the bear crushing together, forming a heavy mass like a stone in her center.

It must be agony. Why didn't she cry out? Why didn't she roar?

And then it was over. Sigrid's arms were full of fur, but the figure inside the fur was much smaller than it had been. As she shifted, the fur remained still in Sigrid's arms, even as the body moved, turning this way and that.

Then she remembered the woman.

Sigrid drew back, nearly falling on her little pile of leaves. A moment later, the woman sat up, holding her fur around her, though Sigrid didn't know whether it was for warmth or for modesty. She hadn't thought anything of it before, but the woman had been nude beneath the bear fur. She knew how a naked body moved in her arms, especially a woman's naked body. This woman wore nothing at all but her two skins.

Sigrid's cheeks burned. She was glad it was too dark for the woman to see her.

"I saw you," Sigrid said.

"I know." The woman's voice was low and husky, almost a growl. It sounded disused, but then who would she have spoken to? The only one she'd been able to keep company with was Sigrid, and she had always been well asleep before dark. "You told me."

"It wasn't only that time. It was many times. I even saw you sleeping once." Sigrid didn't know why she was confessing all of this, or why it came out in such a rush. It felt like a secret she had no purpose keeping, and she wanted it out of her as soon as she could manage it. "I started to think you only became a woman when I was asleep, or only at night."

"The second." She was smiling; Sigrid could hear it in her voice, even though it was too dark for her to make out anything on her face. "It's a curse that was laid on me years ago. By day, I am a great bear. Only by night do I become myself again." Her voice turned bitter. "It's why I wander the mountains. There aren't many who would welcome a bear, no matter how gentle I try to make myself."

Sigrid shivered and told herself it was the cold. "What's your name?"

"I don't know." She sighed. "It's been long enough that I hardly remember what people call me. So often it's 'brown one' or 'honey-eater'. Do you really want a name for me?"

"If we speak more like this, yes." If she became a woman at night, with a tongue and a mind, they would have many chances to talk over winter, until the days grew long again. Sigrid couldn't imagine a conversation passing without names.

Besides, she wanted to roll the woman's name over her tongue. It had been so long since she had done that with anyone. She missed it almost as much as she missed fresh bread.

The woman sighed again. "Call me Ursula, I suppose. It's as good a name as any."

"Ursula."

Sigrid hadn't meant for the name to slip past her lips. It should have been a thought, something even less than a whisper. Instead, it seemed to drift through the chilly air, settling beside Ursula, wrapping itself around her.

Ursula crept closer to her. "What's your name?" she asked.

"S-Sigrid." She bit her lip, cursing herself for the stammer. She really was cold. It wasn't just a faint excuse.

At once, Ursula was by her side, wrapping the warm bearskin around the both of them. Sigrid hadn't realized she was nearly naked herself until Ursula was right next to her, but suddenly all she could think of was her skin beside Ursula's, both of them warm and alive and human all at the same time.

"Why are you here, Sigrid? What curse was laid on you?"

"I was banished."

Ursula laid a rough hand on her knee, and again, everything spilled out. Sigrid could no more have stopped it than she could have stopped the snowmelt in spring.

"I'm a thief. Always have been. Usually it's just small things, bits and pieces to prove I can, or to get a little extra money. I take things no one will notice going missing. At least, I thought I did, but then I was found with a silver ring. I was banished instead of being hanged, and I suppose that's good, but…" But she hadn't wanted to be banished in the first place. She hadn't wanted to have a part of herself stripped from her. "Before, I could become a bird. There was a part of me that was a great eagle. There was nothing I loved more than to find a warm current of air that would lift me up so high I should have felt dizzy from it."

Ursula wrapped an arm around Sigrid's shoulders, drawing her close. "It isn't so bad, being only human," she said. "Sometimes I wish I could be again."

Sigrid leaned her head against Ursula's shoulder. It would be so easy to kiss her. They were so close to one another just now.

She didn't. She only took Ursula's free hand between her own, feeling the calluses with her own callused fingers. "What is it like to be a bear?" she asked. "I've known some who could become one, but they rarely did." It was bad luck, everyone said, though finding a bear had been very good luck for her. She couldn't have survived without Ursula.

"To be a bear," Ursula mused. "I feel... powerful. As though I can do anything at all, but there's nothing I need to do. I'm strong and I'm sturdy. As long as no one bothers me, I don't need to bother them." She laughed, a low barking sound. "It helps that most people keep their distance. I don't think I've met a single person who would want to bother me."

"It must be nice," Sigrid said. "Being so secure."

"It can be. It's also lonely." Ursula shifted. Sigrid could feel every single muscle in her body. "I will let you stay with me through winter. Past winter, if you're willing."

Sigrid had never felt such desperation before, and never before had she felt it soothed like this. She felt as though Ursula's words were running all through her, just under her skin.

"I'll need clothes," Sigrid said. "I don't know how you manage with nothing but a bearskin, but I'm sure I'll freeze."

"Don't worry," said Ursula. "I'll find you something. If nothing else, we can always steal a dress and cloak."

Sigrid laughed and nestled beside Ursula beneath the bear

skin. She would have to wake before dawn; she didn't know what would happen if she was still wrapped up in the skin when morning came and the curse took hold once more. Still, for now, she would sleep. Everything else could be worried over later.

For now, she was safe.

PETER VANGELDEREN

Peter VanGelderen has made his home in Rochester Hills in his native state of Michigan, where he is surrounded by creative friends. During the day, he assists small business merchants with their credit card processing, but on nights and weekends, he is either writing or editing his fantasy novel or short stories.

He uses his experience from studying psychology at Kalamazoo College to create characters who reflect both the healthy and toxic aspects of human behavior. When taking a break from writing, Peter spends his time absorbing stories from other books and television series to broaden his creative mind.

Peter's stories have been a part of two DSP anthologies, first with *Wolves* in *Reign of Queens*, and then again with *Below* in *Lethal Impact*. He is very excited to share the story of *Bear* in *Spirit*.

BEAR

PETER VANGELDEREN

Apainter sat alone on the hilltop. Beetles and toads gibbered desultory songs from within the pond at the base of the knoll. The birds had left, taking their soprano notes with them, leaving the swampy orchestra sounding a bit lower than usual. With the rhythmic babbling of the creeks that fed the pond, the music of the afternoon relaxed the painter's bones and helped them work. As the sunlight flared to the deep orange of late day, they frowned. Only a few hours of good light remained to work.

Bear glared at the steady flow of the pond. Water was their nemesis. They had little trouble with trees and bushes. Grass was a simple matter of careful, short brushstrokes. Even animals weren't a problem, so long as they held still for long enough. But Bear hated painting water. For whatever reason, the waves and intricacies of a creek or pond always looked unnatural on the canvas.

If one were to come across Bear on that hillock, they'd see an enormously tall figure menacingly scribbling with a paintbrush that appeared comically small clutched in colossal fingers. Shifters were uncommon in these marshy northern forests, and those shifters of ursine blood were no exception. However, Bear was large even for their kind. An onlooker would see a massive bulb of deep umber hair tied behind the painter's head, as well as large braids of thick beard falling from their chin. They might think the mystery artist wore a scratchy black shirt. They'd be wrong, for that was simply more hair, or perhaps fur, as that would be a more appropriate term. Then, after a moment, someone who came across this giant painter might decide to retreat upon spotting the massive greataxe stuck into the ground a few feet away.

Bear wouldn't mind someone wandering nearby, so long as they stayed quiet. Although they did mind the sudden scream that shattered the serenity of the wilderness. They grit their teeth, hoping it was just an isolated sound that wouldn't multiply. After a few seconds, their frustration climbed as more screams followed, joined with the sounds of clashing metal and ghastly groans. Bear growled, their wild eyebrows shifting to an angry slant. Excessive noise was one of the few things that could throw off their process. The painter would get no more practice tonight.

They stood, storing their supplies and lumbering over to the axe. With slight effort, they wrenched the great weapon from the dirt, feeling the knobs of the wooden handle as they slung the hulking stone blade over their shoulder.

They muttered in a voice of rolling boulders, "Damned undead."

The village was already burning. Evil arrows steeping in oil and fire had struck the thatch roofs of the three buildings closest to the forest's edge. A meager militia group had formed to stop the raider's advance, but the few old farmers and teenagers with pitchforks and hunting knives were woefully outnumbered. Three had already been wounded, with one approaching death as a healer struggled to stem the flow of blood.

Opposite the villagers marched a band of monsters that were much too common in this cursed world. The dead, both fresh and old, had risen to wreak havoc on the living world. Barely rotted zombies shuffled side-by-side ancient skeletons whose souls had departed centuries ago. The walking corpses, afflicted by the clumsiness of still-petrifying flesh, limped resiliently toward the fearful humans. Those creatures who'd rotted down to their bones carried crude weapons, loosing arrows and grasping spears and short swords in cold, white fingers.

One of the village defenders flung a spade at the monstrous entities, reeling back as if throwing a javelin. The metal tip of the tool soared through the air and buried itself nicely in a zombie's bloated chest. The fiend slammed into the ground from the force. The defender cheered for a moment before the monster rose back to its feet in defiance, resuming its steady pace.

Bear strode up to the battlefield, letting their irritation flow through their legs and arms. Now properly annoyed, they charged into the undead army's flank, bringing the head of their axe down on the closest zombie. The power behind the blow obliterated the upper portion of the creature's body, spraying thick, amber ichor over the grass. Another blow to the thing's body crushed what little unlife remained.

Seeing the new threat, the ghouls turned to Bear. Over a dozen of these creatures shambled to attack as the skeletons in the back-line prepared themselves. Such a force would easily overwhelm a normal soldier and prove a match to all but the mightiest warriors. However, Bear was one of the mightiest warriors. Not only blessed with the strength of their blood, but they also wielded a decade of experience in dealing with the constant threat of the living dead.

Bear slashed again, sending two more sprawling into their rotting companions. Another blow cleaved one in half. Then, bellowing with the rumble of an earthquake, Bear swept a zombie's legs, taking them off below the knee and finishing the job with a weighty stomp. As the painter swung, they created a canvas of rotting bodies and brown sludge, although the style was not one of realism and much more in the abstract.

One managed to rip at the shifter's arm, scratching a shallow cut into their fur. Fury flowed into Bear, fueling a transition to their primal form. Their fur grew suddenly longer, their teeth sharpened and enlarged, and the lower portion of their face suddenly jutted out to a snout. With a newly clawed fist, Bear grasped the zombie that had dared to touch them and lifted them into the air with one arm. They roared with vengeance, slamming the creature into the last group of its comrades and sending them all broken into the mud. A hew of the greataxe followed, then another, and nearly a dozen more after that, each strike punctuated by a guttural yell. When the final blow fell, none of the corpses moved again.

At this point, Bear came to notice the pair of arrows stuck in their back, as well as the one in their thigh. Though the arrowheads were no more painful than splinters, they would be punished. Turning toward the skeletons, Bear charged again. Two of the bonemen rushed to meet the artist head-on, brandishing round metal shields and stout blades. The artist lowered their shoulder and tackled the nearest of them at full force. The metal of the shield collapsed, and the power surged through the autonomous bones. The skeleton shattered. Its pieces exploded in all directions, one of the flying femurs even taking out the leg of one of the undead archers.

The second enemy's shield was no match for Bear's axe. The hefty stone blade nearly tore the rusted metal in two, tearing off the undead's arm in the process. Another swing smashed through the bare ribs and felled the remaining pieces into a heap. An arrow struck Bear's chest. They growled as they ripped it from their flesh, eyes flaring open to see the archer knocking another projectile. Baring their teeth, Bear reeled back with the greataxe and stepped forward, throwing the great weapon at the ranged attacker. The axe spun through the air, picking up speed until it found purchase on the skeleton's skull. With a forceful crack, the blade crushed through bone, the boneman burst, and the weapon buried itself in the mud beyond its now splattered target.

Bear did not need the weapon. A trio of boney spearmen moved forward, and the painter sidestepped towards their flank. The nearest member of the osseous phalanx lunged at Bear, but they easily evaded the point, taking the opportunity to dash forward. Trying desperately to backpedal, the skeleton clamored into one of its squad mates. Bear thrust their hand through the former spearman toward the one behind and yanked, jamming the two bonemen together until their ribs were interlocked and wedged together. The duo pushed and pulled fruitlessly to separate from each other while Bear firmly gripped their spines. With hairy muscles clenched and a roar that thundered through the forest, the shifter tore them both asunder. Before the pieces even had a chance to settle, Bear grasped the final spearman by the collarbone and jerked the boneman forward into a headbutt. They repeated the process, slamming their forehead into the skull once, twice, thrice, four times in rapid succession, leaving the skeleton's head a crumbling mess.

Now, only two of the lifeless marauders remained, mindlessly loosing arrows at the giant tearing through their ranks. Bear charged them, ducking beneath their projectiles. One grazed their hip, but that only fueled their rage. The shifter kept low, and upon reaching the final bonemen, went even lower. With a huge hand, Bear swept the archer off its feet, hoisting it into the air by its ankles. Spinning for momentum, they hurled the grappled skeleton directly at the other archer. The undead missile crashed into the last boneman, sending both tumbling into shards. Bear bellowed again, this time toward the sky in victory.

Panting, they moved toward their axe, still firmly set in the mud. As the cheering from the townsfolk swelled, Bear frowned. They could do without the noise and they certainly would have preferred to figure out how to paint that damn pond, but a good fight is a good fight. Of course, even though they take great measures to stay out of the business of humans, saving some lives still gives them a warm feeling in the depths of their gut. Bear slung the weapon over their shoulder, looking back at the villagers pumping their fists, rejoicing to the heavens, and beckoning them over. With a small sigh, they started for the settlement. They'd get no more painting done today anyway, and they'd never turn down free food.

THE BONFIRE CRACKLED, CREATING A SNAPPING PERCUSSION TO the half-drunken verses of unfamiliar songs. Voices blared into the night air, very much out of tune and completely unconcerned about that fact. A low haze covered the villagers, lit by the flaring firelight. The sweet, sour smell of spilled mead and ale merged with the savory smoke and meat. Bear enjoyed that, at least. Most of the meat they ate was barely cooked, mostly just crisped for a skin. A nicely smoked turkey leg was a treat. Unfortunately, that was about the only delight the celebration had to offer.

The boozy merrymakers were naturally friendly to the village's hero, but their hospitality was heavily tinted with aggression. Almost a dozen times now Bear had to refuse an offer of some kind of alcohol, and each time they were met with an incredulous look and an insistence to try what they'd already politely declined. Several had shrugged and shook their heads as if Bear had been the rude one in the conversation. A few had even scowled at the hairy painter, clearly holding back contempt-laced words and bared teeth. Strange that their attitudes could grow so bitter during a party in Bear's honor. Naturally, they wouldn't attempt to start a brawl with the one who'd singlehandedly torn apart an undead platoon, but in this village, many would prefer to avoid having a shifter within their midst at all. Bear's refusal to drink, although it had nothing to do with their animal blood, was simply another difference they could petulantly fixate on.

The assertiveness of the supposedly welcoming townsfolk would only get worse as the night went on. As they continually shot down drinks to an increasingly irritated and irritating parade of oafs who were offended simply by the word "no," the villagers started to give them a wider and wider berth. Normally, this would have been wonderful, but the newfound privacy caused other problems. Partway through their second turkey leg, Bear looked up to see a woman approaching. On her face was a smug smirk. From her scalp grew long hair in curls. Upon her midsection was what must have been an incredibly uncomfortable dress. Within her eyes was a look that immediately put Bear on alert.

"Mind if I join you?" she said, a twinkle in her eye.

Bear grunted and took another bite of the bird.

The woman, somehow, took that as an invitation. "My name is Anna. What may I call you?"

"Bear cares not." The painter said, not taking their eyes off their meal.

She chuckled and leaned much too close. "A simple man."

"Not a man." Bear scowled.

Anna's brow furrowed. "Not a...I'm sorry I don't understand."

"Not a man," Bear repeated. "Nor a woman. Bear is bear."

Her face let out a laugh of realization. "Oh, you're a shifter! Of course!" She put an unwelcome hand on Bear's leg. "I apologize. I hope I can make it up to you."

They pulled their leg away with an annoyed growl. "You are incorrect. Shifters can be men. They can also be women. However, Bear is neither."

Anna's face scrunched up again. "I'm afraid I don't understand."

"That is of no concern to Bear."

She let out a nervous laugh, shaking her head with condescension. "I'm just trying to flirt with you, honey. I don't mean to upset you."

"Bear knows what you are trying to do, and could tell from the moment you walked over," the painter said. "You are not subtle. Bear has no interest in what you're offering."

Anna scoffed, placing an appalled hand on her chest. "Oh, I'm sorry, am I not good enough for you? Or do you want one of the menfolk to court you, is that what you want?"

"Bear wants to eat."

"What are you even?"

They met the woman's eyes, narrowing their own. "An artist."

"What kind of person isn't interested in women nor

men?" She glared at them, leaning back in her chair and folding her arms.

Bear shrugged and answered honestly, "Bear."

"I can't believe this," the woman huffed and stormed off. As she walked away, Bear could hear her mutter. "Fucking freak."

Left in a particularly ornery state, Bear decided that they'd take another few turkey legs and head back to their campsite in the forest. They wondered why they'd even bother to save the village. A couple of minutes and a drumstick passed when another woman approached their table. They were nearing the time to leave, but this one had a different look about her. Her blonde hair was tied up. She was shy, a bit intimidated, perhaps, but meant no manipulation and bore no selfishness. Bear didn't mind such people.

"I'm sorry to bother you," the woman said, peering at them with warm brown eyes, "but that woman who just stormed off, did you reject her?"

Bear nodded, curious but cautious.

"Wow. Not a man in the village who'd do that. A few women who wouldn't either." She gazed across the fire at Anna, who was now chatting with a random village man. "Not me, that's for sure."

Bear cocked their head. "What is your name?"

"Estelle," she replied. "And you?"

"Bear. Did you need something?"

Her eyes went a little wide at the bluntness of the question. "Well, no, not exactly. I heard what happened. I came to thank you for saving us and I ended up eavesdropping a little, if I'm being honest."

Bear raised an eyebrow.

She stumbled over her next words. "Sorry, I shouldn't have listened in. I know what it's like, though, at least to a certain extent. People like me aren't exactly looked fondly upon here either. You looked lonely, so if you want, you can come to sit with us over there." She pointed toward a lonely table of villagers, set aside from the rest and largely ignored by everyone else in the celebration. Only some of them had drinks, and for the most part, they were laughing and chatting in their small group. One of them was even hunched over a canvas with a brush, quietly listening to the group and occasionally entering the conversation with a smile. Bear lifted their head.

"Bear has no interest in drinking, flirting, loudly singing, pretty much all of what is happening here tonight. Right now, that table looks to be the most enjoyable place in this village. Lead the way."

Estelle smiled, leading Bear to her friends. As the pair approached, the others stared wide-eyed at the hulking shifter. The painter scanned them, feeling itches falling up and down their back.

Estelle broke the tension. "This is Bear. They want to join us."

"Hello," Bear said, waving a massive and stiff arm.

"Have a seat!" A youth with a wide-brimmed hat and a big smile gestured toward an empty chair.

As Bear sat, Estelle tapped them on the shoulder. "So, Bear, this is Tom, Delilah-" As she spoke, she gestured toward the youth with the wide-brimmed hat, next to a person with short, cropped hair and thick but trimmed brows. "And Steel," she indicated the man in the hooded cloak with gloved hands wrapped around a mug of ale, "and finally Jesse." She finished with the oldest person, who was carefully finishing a painting of a lake during a windstorm. Bear's eyes went wide at the stunning brushwork, but they were still feeling a bit too awkward to give voice to their admiration.

Bear nodded to the group.

"Can I get you a drink, Bear?" asked Steel, holding up his cup of ale.

Bear shook their head, getting rigidly tense as they started to think this may have been a mistake. "Bear does not drink."

The hooded one bobbed his head with understanding. "Ok, let me know if you change your mind."

"Be aware," Tom leaned in with a smirk, "he doesn't actually want you to change your mind. He wants all the ale to himself."

"Well, naturally!" Steel splayed their arms on the table in front of him, "but that doesn't mean I'm not going to offer!"

Bear chuckled for the first time that night. "Thank you, Steel."

The tension began to fade. That was certainly the best exchange the artist had ever experienced when it came to declining booze. As the others returned to their chatting, a certain peacefulness descended on the group. Even though the topics of conversation were completely chaotic sometimes, they never strayed to toxicity. Never did someone mention how much they hate this group or that. Not once did someone shame another for a hobby or unchangeable and arbitrary physical feature. Bear was still more interested in eating than in speaking, but for once, they didn't resent the noise.

A half-hour passed like this, with Bear eating their turkey and listening to the waxing and waning discussions. For a good ten minutes, they all were discussing their nearly unanimous love of cheese. Except for Delilah, though, they became ill from it. That, of course, was inconvenient, as they lived on a dairy farm. Then, somehow, the conversation moved to Estelle's lute strings, and how they needed to be replaced soon. Unfortunately, the village was not slaughtering sheep this time of year, and therefore she would not be able to get the required gut to make more strings. Bear joined the conversation for the first time at this point, stating that at their camp they had some spare sheep's gut Estelle could use. The group nervously glossed over the fact that someone just had spare sheep's gut lying around, and Estelle thanked them. At one point, Delilah casually stole Tom's hat. Often, the group would begin to reference some inside joke or mutual acquaintance that Bear couldn't relate to, but they found those were great times to wolf down more turkey.

"Say, Bear," Steel asked after a particularly scintillating conversation about the benefits of naming your cows.

Bear looked up from a half-eaten turkey leg, finishing the rest of the massive bit they'd taken.

"I notice you rarely use 'me' or 'I.' You like to refer to yourself as Bear. Why is that?"

"Bear is an artist." Bear shrugged. "That is what great artists do."

Jesse, who hadn't spoken since saying hello, suddenly burst out into laughter. The group, including Bear, joined shortly after.

"They're right!" Jesse gasped between chortles, "All the best ones do! We have no idea why!"

The rest of the evening only continued to improve. Bear started to joke more often, smile more often, let out deep, roaring guffaws more often. For one of the first times in their life, they enjoyed being around people. With a mountain of bones in front of them and a chuckle in their voice, Bear felt their soul grow. Happiness could be found in the satisfaction of a good day's work on a painting, or after a thrilling battle, but never once had it come from spending time with others.

As the night wore on, Bear noticed Jesse's painting was becoming increasingly fantastic. They couldn't take their eyes off the intricate white caps on the waves. Jesse's technique seemed effortless; the motion so elegant yet simple. The colors were perfect, mixed right there on the canvas itself, the chaos of the swirling shades adding texture to the raging waves. Bear had to know how this master gained such skill.

"Jesse?" Bear asked, trying and failing to make their voice sound less rocky.

The hunched painter raised their head, eyes wide with concentration.

"How do you create such majesty?"

Jesse blushed and looked away, stammering, "Well, I wouldn't exactly call it majesty...I can't get this wave quite right and the clouds aren't dark enough and the shading is certainly not my best work-"

Bear leaned forward. "It's beautiful," they asserted, unable to take their eyes off the canvas. "Bear cannot imagine making such a thing. How do you get the waves so...wavy?"

Still blushing, Jesse shrugged. "Well, it's not that hard, really. You could easily do better, I'm sure."

The shifter scoffed, "No, Bear cannot paint water, nor sky. You are the better artist."

"To tell you the truth," Jesse bowed, "This is all I can do. The reason all I paint is water is because I'm completely lost when it comes to land. I can't do grass or rocks or trees, nothing but water. This is all I can do."

Bear stroked their long, wild beard. They could easily paint trees. Rocks and grass were even easier. They began to giggle.

"Friend, Bear can help you with that. If you help me with water."

Jesse's blush faded, replaced with a surprised smile. "I think I can do that."

The pair of painters spent the next hour dragging brushes

on a blank canvas. They created a forest of mismatched trees, some merely blank twigs stuck in the ground, others a perfect imitation of mother earth's creations, and everything in between. They made boulders ranging from round blobs of grey to flawless sculptures and grass of all textures. A river flowed through this strange world, magically blending into the greenery on one bank and clumsily smashing into the rest of the world on the other. The two of them showed clear improvement with the other's guidance, making the overall landscape a jumble of patchwork styles. Despite the unorthodoxy of the painting, it was immediately one of Bear's favorites.

The evening continued, Bear completely unaware of the other villagers that weren't sitting at the table with their new friends. The noise around them lessened, the light from the bonfires began to fade, and the smells of smoke and ale and meat became stale in the air. Bear bit into their final leg of turkey, the meat now cold from exposure to the night's wind. The smiles from the others had fallen from elated to peaceful and content. Their eyes sagged with the bags from too long without sleep. Bear's hair fell in knots. The thick fur on their chest and arms was disheveled, even more so than usual. Time had caught up with them, and now was the time to finally retire.

"Alright," Bear sat up, rubbing their eyes, "The night is done. Back to the woods for me."

The others nodded with yawns and tired faces. However, they all added their own sighs of disappointment.

"Until next time," Tom said, stretching. "Say goodbye to Real Tom, back to Tom who likes women."

Bear scrunched their face. "What?"

"You know, the 'Tom' my parents think I am." The young man tried to laugh the statement off, but there was a sadness in his voice that he couldn't hide.

"Why do your parents not know who you are? Bear does not understand."

The rest of the group glanced at each other nervously. Steel took another swig of ale, this one deeper than normal. Jesse and Delilah avoided Bear's eyes. Tom sucked his teeth. Estelle wrapped her fingers around themselves, tightening her grip like a patient bites a bit of wood while getting a wound sewn.

"See, you know how I mentioned we aren't looked upon fondly by the people here?" She began, "That includes our parents. We know they don't approve of us, so we have to hide ourselves. If they found out, we can't count on them being supportive. We can't even count on them to not turn violent."

"My mother would lash out with a pan, I know that. Ring me like a bell." Tom tried to giggle to soften the horrifying nature of the statement. Bear tensed.

Delilah spoke next, her face darkening. "My da wouldn't beat me, I don't think, but he'd still force me into marriage to some man who could help elevate his status." Her eyes grew wet. "I might be lucky enough to get stuck with someone who's as uninterested in lovemaking as I am, then after a kid or two, we'd be done with it." A flicker of hope came onto her face, but quickly faded. "Gods know that's probably not happening, though."

"They're not going to attempt to marry me if they find out who I am," Steel gazed forward, unblinking and downcast. "There was someone a few towns over, born looking like a man but being a woman. When she tried to live as she really was, her parents were outraged…" They paused. Their voice had dulled and their face went blank as if they weren't even there anymore. "I don't need to tell you what happened to her. When the news reached my parents, they were disappointed. Not at the treatment of the woman, mind you, but feeling sorry for the parents. I could see it in their eyes, though, if they were in the same situation, they'd do the same thing. The only reason I can wear this," he gestured to his rough spun cloak and pants, "is because I always go to Jesse's after leaving home to change. I won't try to wear pants and a man's shirt in front of my parents. This is the only time I can be me, be Steel. At home, I have to become Sandra, the woman my parents think I am, and if they find out I'm not that woman, they'll kill me."

Bear's jaw fell. "So, the hood…"

"To make sure no one recognizes me." Steel's face slowly looked to Jesse, his eyes watery. "Thank the Gods for Jesse. Without them, I'd probably have been caught already."

Jesse nodded, "The village still thinks of me as a man, and I do like women, so I can pass. They still only tolerate me because I'm the only butcher in town. If another showed up and decided to live here, I don't know how much longer I'd be welcome."

"We're stuck," Estelle frowned, "There are other towns out there that aren't so bigoted, and the bigger cities are easier to vanish and reappear in, but we have no way to reach them. None of us can survive in the wilderness and our parents won't fund traveling by convoy and living somewhere else."

As Bear heard the tales of their friends, confusion settled on their face. They had been raised by their mother, a woman who cared not who Bear married, nor what they called themselves. She loved them, taught them survival skills, nurtured their health both physical and mental. The thought of a parent treating their children like this started as a red point in Bear's mind and grew to a billowing fire. Confusion and disbelief turned to rage. Bear's teeth grew to their ursine length, their snout expanded slightly, and their hair started to grow without their permission. They had to take a few deep breaths and close their eyes to control the surging wrath.

A hand gripped Bear's shoulder. They opened their eyes to see Estelle, a look of concern and support on her face.

"It's ok, we got each other," she said with a weak smile.

"It's monstrous." Bear scowled as their features returned to their more human appearance.

"It is," she agreed as the others nodded, "but we manage."

"You shouldn't have to," Bear growled. "No *person* should ever treat others in such a way. The fact that your *parents* are the worst offenders makes things even worse."

"It does. The world is cruel," Steel muttered.

"The world is not cruel." Bear said, "The world is full of good. Singing birds, peaceful hills and forests, a good turkey leg, friends, and love. These demons are the ones who are cruel."

"I'm sure they love us still," Tom ran a hand through his hair. "Deep down at least."

"No." Bear shook their head, their massive hands turning into hairy fists. "Not love. Perhaps that is what they think it is, but it has become so corrupted by hate that it is love no longer. No one can claim they love a child they would hurt simply for being who they are. They do not know what love is, and likely never will."

Bear spat their words with anger, "As bad as the undead, they are! Beasts! And I know beasts! They do not deserve you." They bared their teeth, "They deserve to be torn to pieces! Bear wants to tear them apart, and cleave through anyone who gets in the way!"

The rest of the group stared at Bear with wide eyes and fearful expressions. Bear took another deep breath, realizing that his love for his new friends had perhaps made them a bit too violent. They rubbed the anger from their eyes and calmed themselves.

"Apologies. Bear will not interfere in your lives without your consent. " Bear met their eyes and cursed their lack of control. "These concepts are new to me, and my temper grew too wild. 'Tis the blood of the Bear."

"You are not the one at fault," Delilah grasped Bears hand. "This is how all should react to such things."

"Agreed," added Steel. "It's actually nice to have such fervent support."

The group chuckled, and not in a forced, sad way, but in relief. Bear squeezed Delilah's hand back and lifted their furry chin.

"Then support is what you shall get," they declared. "If your birth givers refuse to rise to the task, then Bear shall do it. Bear will stay in the forest nearby to be close. If any of you must flee, Bear will protect you and teach you the ways of survival. Bear loves you as you deserve to be loved, values you for your true worth, as you ought to be. If needed, Bear shall be there in a moment's notice, but the axe will not be raised unless needed." They wagged a finger at them. "But rest assured, if Bear must fight for you, Bear will. Of that, you need not doubt."

Tears began to flow from every eye there. Bear gestured, their colossal arms out wide, and the group huddled in, all holding each other within Bear's protective hug. With a gentle squeeze, Bear brought them closer.

"Hey," Estelle said, her voice slightly cracking, "you're our Mama Bear!"

The group laughed through the tears, Bear's gravelly voice the loudest by far.

BAREND NIEUWSTRATEN III

Barend Nieuwstraten III has been primarily working on a collection of works set within a single fantasy world as well as a series of science-fiction pieces.

He is currently working on stories ranging from flash fiction and short stories to stand alone novels and an epic series.

Learn more at Twitter.com/Barend666

CHILDREN OF BRECHOR

BAREND NIEUWSTRATEN III

E thela placed an acorn into her father's hands, resting lifelessly over his chest. She took in the smell of the freshly burrowed earth of his shallow grave and brushed his thick, light-brown hair back. "Fairwell, Lion," she said. "Mightiest of us all."

Throm offered his hand from above. She didn't need it, but took it all the same. She'd never seen him so sad. As the others pushed the dirt in, she looked around her. Eight, there now were. Eight, including herself. Eight, including Antos, who was not truly one of them, but an adoptive part of their family. Though, with her father now dead, she was the last of her blood family.

"May your tree grow tall, great lion," Throm said, as the earth was closed upon their leader. "May you find your way fast to the Endless Wilds to hunt at Brechor's side. Ethold, father to us all, in heart." Throm was a large man, but not too big to suffer grief. A robust figure of black messy hair that covered his head and face, he closed his eyes and placed his great fist over his own heart. All present did the same.

They had a long silence together before they began to

look at each other. The question of who would lead them next was on everyone's minds, but all were loath to start the conversation so soon. Ethela looked to her druidic kin. Throm was the strongest. Especially when he took the bear form, but even when he didn't. A strong shifter seemed a natural choice, to replace the one they had lost. Though that brought the choice back to her as well.

"Let us then speak of what must be spoken and be done with it," Hralda, the bird caller, finally said. Nearing fifty, she was the oldest and wisest of them. Her hair, having greyed long before its time, only made her seem all the more so, despite her otherwise youthful build. "Who amongst us should lead us next?"

"Does not the duty pass down as it does with lords and kings?" Antos asked, pointing to Ethela. A soldier of the Sond empire, on the wrong side of the Kestrian Empire's brutal expansion, he was cut off from his kind, but still harbored their ways.

"If Ethela will take the mantel willingly, there are none here who would challenge her," Hralda said. "Will the mighty boar replace the lion?"

"I took after my father, becoming a shifter, but sadly not my mother," Ethela said. "Had I become a healer, like her, this decision would not need to be made."

"We each choose our own path and you chose the one right for you," Hralda counselled. "Your mother, Mirella, encouraged you on that path. It was not folly to fail to anticipate her untimely demise, nor a failing to lack the clairvoyance to choose a path that would have saved your father. You can accept no blame nor question your own judgment on these matters."

"Perhaps," Ethela said. "But as one who stands before you and questions it, does that not, perhaps, reveal a lack of leadership?"

"It does if you believe it does," the bird caller conceded. "Then who? Throm?" she said, pointing to the large man. "Our changelings," she gestured towards Breht, half man, half stag, with segmented legs of a beast and antlers that sprouted wide from his head. Hralda's hand move towards Grola, the goat, who, like her lover, had taken the path of half-beast. Goat horns turning up and back from the top of her brow with her long ears that twitched as she shook her head. Neither would rise to leader, for their nature was too like the beasts they had partially become. Though brave in battle, they were timid in discourse.

Flohs Eathernheart stepped forward, a man whose forearms and fists were long stained dark from the earth, burying them often in dirt to speak with the trees. Even the veins, beneath the skin of his arms, seemed green. He saw far through land by tree as Hralda did through air by birds. He raised his darkened hand towards Valris Oakenflesh, the other, amongst them, who embraced the trees. By pointing to another, he had passed consideration. All knew his heart belonged to Valris, even though hers belonged to Ethela. So, in choosing one of his own kind and one whom he loved, his cast would be twice questioned in the minds of the rest. As her lover, Ethela was hesitant to agree, though she did in her heart. Another voice would need to speak.

"Yes," Throm said, of the woman who could will her flesh as hard as wood. "Valris is both wise and brave and, after Ethela, was closest to Ethold. I would follow her gladly."

Ethela nodded, free now to do so as the changelings agreed. Antos, the soldier, also nodded and smiled.

"Then I name Valris Oakenflesh our new leader," Hralda said, who was already their leader in many ways. She had been the heart of their group where Ethold had been the mind. No decision was made without her blessing, and that was unlikely to change.

"You flatter me," Valris said. "And I cannot refuse if you all agree so." She was a pale woman, often shielded from the sun by her proximity to the trees from which she drew her power, and the hardening of her flesh seemed to keep her from tanning. She was thin but strong, contoured by muscle like Flohs, but not large like Throm, or even Ethela, the strongest of the women in build.

"How close is the legion?" Antos asked Flohs, who buried his fists into the earth beneath them. He closed the eyes on his face to see with the eyes of the forest. "They are camped for the time being," he said. "Scouting parties are active but traveling far at the moment."

"Damn them and their grey metal," Antos muttered, with his hand on the hilt of his bronze sword. "I will take one of their magic swords the next time we meet, I swear it."

"Their swords are not magic," Hralda corrected the soldier. "Their swords are the opposite of magic. This iron they forge for swords, knives, and cladding upon their centurions. It is a metal most unprecious, lacking the grace and beauty of bronze and copper before it. It does not recognize the might of magic and even thwarts it, as we have seen."

"I have seen," Antos said, looking west in memory. His olive skin and oily black hair that was quick to curl, was a constant reminder of how far from home he'd been driven by the might of the new empire. He was far further east than his own, once mighty, empire had ever conquered. A lone survivor separated by kingdoms from his own kind. "Witches fought beside us, when we faced these Kestrians, spreading across Edenya. They wounded our most powerful witches by merely driving their iron daggers and swords into their footprints, left in the dirt. Though they bled not, it was as if the blades were driven into their flesh."

"I can see why you believed it to be magic," Hralda said,

with sudden realization as she pondered a moment. "Witches draw their magic from nature as do we, but in a less harmonious manner that taxes them more. The iron will not harm us in this way, for I have seen them try. Until you spoke of this, I did not understand. I did not know what I was seeing at the time, when they stabbed at the ground in pursuit as they hunted us. A most terrible advantage to have over our dark distant cousins in magic."

"We must adapt our methods," Valris said. "For not so long ago, there were thirteen of us, before even Antos joined us." She approached the soldier and pointed to his sword. "At one time, bronze was the new metal."

"The iron of the Kestrians has pushed back the Sond," Antos said, "as the bronze of the Edes before us drove the Basiarli to extinction, after their copper conquered the first men and drove back the orcs who dared come west with their weapons of stone and wood."

"But both the Sond and the Edes used bronze," Valris said. "Your people scattered their empire to the wind with the same metal that clad their flesh and filled their hands. So, there's something to be said for tactics. And all who brought something new still suffered losses, did they not?"

"We are in retreat, though," Ethela reminded her lover. "We are now on the wrong side of the Spine of Gods," she said, of the great mountain range that separated the kingdom of Westmeer from the rest of the continent of Edenya. "None of the empires, Antos speaks of, have ever come this far east."

"We must have brothers and sisters in this land," Throm said. "We may find more of our kind here."

"We've barely had time to consider such a task so far," Valris said, being thrust fast into her new role. "At every spare moment then, I charge Hralda to search from the sky and Flohs to search the lands as far as they may reach, for signs of others like us. But when we face these Kestrians, from now on, it must be when they are in smaller number. They must not see us coming. We must employ more cunning. For at every encounter so far we have been forced to leave the place of battle before we could even claim spoils."

"What spoils do we need?" Breht asked.

"Armed with antlers, you may well ask, but iron swords in your hands would make you deadly," Varlis said. "An iron sword in the hand of a trained soldier like Antos would be a great boon for us."

"Instead of one they could slice through," Antos agreed.

"We will take from them, for all they have taken from us," Valris declared, passionately. "We will replenish and exceed our number. We will make friends with the men of Westmeer, confiscating as many of these Kestrian swords to arm ourselves and hand them over to our new allies so that they may hold back the advancing storm."

Ethela filled with pride hearing the woman she loved stir the others so. They were inspired and reinvigorated. Not just in spite of their grief, but because of it. Vengeance was in their hearts for the loss of Ethela's father, who had led them, her mother, who had healed them, and all the others they had lost along the way.

THE EIGHT BEGAN TO REST DURING THE DAY, WHEN CERTAIN nothing was coming their way, camping early to conserve their strength. Night, they decided, would be when they would work against the invaders. Most of the group were spread wide. Hralda, the bird caller, was asleep in Throm's great arms while the half-beast changelings, Grola and Breht were curled up together, sleeping as woodland creatures do. Flohs slept as he always did, sat up, leaning against a tree trunk.

Ethela laid her head in Valris's lap, who gently stroked her thick brown hair that was longer than it looked, but it's wild unkemptness kept it bunched above her shoulders when she stood. Together they watched Antos practice his sword form. A lone soldier of a falling empire, he was a tragic figure to them, but his uniqueness made him belong to the rest somehow.

"The Basiarli were the first empire of Edenya," Valris said, quietly, as she observed the soldier. "When they fell to the might of the Edes, they were near slain to extinction. The few who survived were kept as slaves, until they too died out over the years. Then the Edes forces, who even thinned the woodelf numbers of Elvaal, tested the northern tribe where Antos's people dwelt. They unleashed a terrible retribution upon themselves and the Sond, realizing their own might, became the third great empire of Edenya. When they enslaved the Edes, the Sondaar made them serve the people of all the lands they conquered to make amends for the destruction the Edes had wrought in their conquest. The Sondaar were cruel to no one else in their reign.

"Famed for their inventiveness in torture though they are, they crushed and belittled no other culture or peoples in their wake. Now the great monster, that is the Kestrian empire, spreads across the land, devouring with iron teeth, biting through earthen magic, and laying paths of flattened rock and stone to its every destination, giving speed to the steps of its replenishing numbers." She continued to watch the soldier practicing his swordsmanship as he patrolled the surrounding woods. "I wonder if his people will survive. Or is he now in the very process of becoming most unique? Like you children of Brechor, becoming half beast as the changelings do or shifting between man and beast at will, but your inner beast chooses you," Valris said, sliding her other hand between her lover's breasts to point to her heart. "Each one unique. In all our travels I never met two shifters or changelings alike. You embody a great boar where you father had been a lion. Throm's mother had been ferocious cat of night-black fur, where he becomes a bear. Flohs, a child of Evanthea like me, connected to the trees, had a mother who thrived in water: a daughter of Enelope."

"There you have commonality," Ethela said, placing her own hand over the one on her chest.

"He communes with the trees through the earth," Valris said. "And not only trees. There is a reason he is named Earthenheart and I am named Oakenflesh. We are as similar as you and Throm."

"I'm sure he would agree with me, if we woke him," Ethela teased.

"He would only agree to be agreeable because he believes he loves me," Valris dismissed.

"Believes?" Ethela questioned the dismissive remark. "I have never seen a truer love, nor could hope to do so."

"That's enough fun-making," Valris said, shaking her head.

"There, I am not," Ethela said, running her hand up Valris's back. "If you were to tell me one day that you no longer felt anything for me, as devastated as I would be, we would grow apart from my end too. My love for you is true, but it comes on the condition that you love me back."

"But I do and always will," Valris said, looking down at her.

"But if we had never slipped into each other's arms, and found each other's hearts, and you had instead professed your love to him, for the rest of your days, my heart would have found another home, eventually. Though I am glad that is not the way of things as they are now, for this was surely meant to be, I don't see myself loving from afar the way he does."

"He loves me because there is no one else to share his

heart," Varlis said. "No one else to distract him. Hralda is old enough to be his mother. Grola is half goat. I am the only woman that provides his eyes somewhere upon which to fall. There are no other worthy options."

Ethela shook her head gently in disagreement. "No. His love is unique and tragic, like Antos. It does not require others to be complete in what it truly is. I think that's beautiful in its own way, don't y..." Ethela trailed off, as something occurred to her. She furrowed her brows. "Wait. What about me? Am I not something on which eyes should fall?"

"I said worthy options," Valris said, suppressing a smile as she slid her hand down to Ethela's belly and squeezed her fingers in to tickle her.

Ethela laughed while trying to feign shock and offense upon her face. She wrestled her in and kissed her. "You better turn your flesh to wood the next time you say something like that."

Antos looked back from his training, smiling amused at the playful display before going back to his sword practice.

"I have missed your smile," Valris told Ethela, brushing her face.

WHEN THEY HAD RESTED FROM THEIR LOSS, THEY WAITED ONE night till the moons where high. Hralda stood with her forearms crossed before her chest. Her eyes were closed so that she could see elsewhere, through the eyes of birds who flew over the enemy camps, looking for the smallest and most vulnerable group to assault. Flohs had his fists buried in the dirt to see what he may, the way he always did. For it was a different sight, as trees had no eyes, as he had once explained to Ethela. The heat of campfires, the breathing of sleeping bodies upon the soil, the vibration of footfalls from patrols. The butchery of beast was felt as blood soaked into the soil, tasted by the roots of that which grew near, as ants marched towards the discarded innards above. The trees that suffered loss of limb, to keep the invaders warm or build barricades, shared their trauma with Flohs.

Together their seers, through earth and sky, agreed upon a small camp to the northwest. A scouting party of eight, building a camp far bigger than they needed. Soon others would join them, so the time to attack was upon the druids who meant to assail them.

Joining hands, they said their druids call in unison. " Evenathea for the things that grow, Enelope for all the waters that flow, Esterine for when we reproduce, Brechor for the beast inside that we let loose, Melenur through whom we mend, and each other whom we must defend, we call upon from all around, until we shall return into the ground."

They approached the site, moving in the shadows of the trees to avoid the light of the campfire ahead. Hralda crossed her arms and closed her eyes. One by one, sleeping birds of the surrounding woodlands woke without song and landed upon the apex of empty tents, nearby branches, rocks, and barricades, perching as they watched the camp from every angle. Little dark eyes giving the bird caller a complete enveloping view.

Flohs dug his hands into the dirt, crouching in the dark. He too shut his eyes, waiting to call upon what he may if the need called for it. Throm slipped out of his clothes, as did Ethela, both breathing quietly as they could manage, naked in the dark, as they allowed their other shape to take form. The transformation was always a discomfort when allowed to happen at its natural pace, painful when rushed, and an agony through which screams could not be silenced when forced as fast as the change could be made. It took years to find the precise place, that dwelt on the threshold of control. All shifters had to find it, as Ethela's father had taught her. To turn as fast as they could within the limits of their own endurance. To know the journey between was as important as either form.

Ethela bent forward as she felt the boar's back muscles slide into place beneath her hardening skin. Thick strands of sparse black hair needled through her shoulders from beneath the surface. She had come far, withstanding what the body could take. It was the jaws, changing the shape of her head, that held her back from changing any faster. The tusks that sprouted, climbing before her eyes then pushing forward. They felt as if they were coming from her throat, the way the pain reached back when they emerged. Turning to see Throm, who preferred leaning against a tree to become the great bear, so that his four paws wouldn't skid on the ground as they grew apart with his increasing size, he was complete before her. As the last part of her human side disappeared, she could force the remainder of the change harder, letting the boar take the pain that she could not have otherwise endured. Turning their shared burden into beastly rage, she was immediately ready to fight.

Valris clenched her fists as a wooden creak emanated from her body. "Now," she said, as her skin adopted a sheen that caught the light of the moons as she began to run towards the camp.

They moved as one. Antos followed Breht and Grola towards the tents, as the great brown bear charged one of the sentries. The ground moved fast under Ethela's trotters, as she charged like a battering ram. Overtaking Throm, she met the Kestrian soldier before he could draw his sword. His skirt of studded leather splints might have protected him against the glancing blows of an enemy sword, but as the tusk of a charging direboar slid up his inner thigh, opening the skin and flesh beneath, an opened artery began to spray his lifeblood in an airborne arc as he was lifted, screaming, off his feet. Ethela knew that no matter what happened next, this man would lose more blood than he could afford to before any could help him. She turned and tossed, to watch him land on the ground.

Panicked, he clutched at his wound, knowing the severity of it. He was forced to draw his sword with the wrong hand, awkwardly trying to get the reach across his own chest to get it out of its scabbard as he gripped it with his thumb on the pommel. She skidded in her tracks, fearful of the grey metal. Looking beyond, Throm was busy, tearing open the throat of the soldier he had pinned down. The bleeding soldier followed her gaze, widening his eyes as he saw what had become of the other sentry. With the flat pommel against his chest, pointing the tip of his gladius at the boar before him, it made an effective deterrent. She dared not risk it.

Grola had leapt through a tent of sleeping soldiers, collapsing it and twisting the slack as she used her backward horns to entangle the support ropes and pull the hammed wooden pegs from the earth. The resting soldiers were like a pair of stolen sheep in a canvas sack, squirming as they woke, trying to make sense of their predicament. But Antos was close behind, driving his bronze sword down, point first.

Breht was pulling away from the next tent, having torn it open with his antlers. Valris was quick to enter, pounding the base of her fists into the waking faces, hard as clubs or cudgels. She beat down with fury, battering and breaking their heads.

Hearing a panicked cry, Ethela's attention was brought back to the soldier she'd wounded, as the black bear, that was Throm, ran past him to another tent, straight into its flaps to screaming men. Roots from nearby trees had made their way through the dirt and sprouted from the ground to pull at the bleeding soldier's arms, pulling them back and down as birds swooped his head. Unable to pinch his leg shut or hold his sword up, Ethela was free to gore him further. She twisted her head as she charged again and slid a tusk into his flank between straps of his chest piece. He made a terrible sound, unable to scream as she found his lung. As she tore free, she saw that their work was done.

When eight dead soldiers were dragged together and accounted for, everything was taken from them. Their armor, bows, arrows with iron tips, iron swords, iron daggers. Their tents were salvaged; the empty ones disassembled and taken, while the torn were used to gather everything. All of it was done while Ethela and Throm lay on the ground. It was the best way to revert, back from beast to man and woman. A process that was never rushed. Two beasts laying on their sides as they puffed deeply, slowing their breathing as they changed a little with each exhale.

By the time they turned back, everything was ready to transport. Their clothes were brought to them by those that loved them and they redressed.

The eight soldiers, stripped of all their garments, were laid naked in a circle around their fire with their heads closest to the pit and their hands joined. Their hearts were cut out and thrown into the fire, while their jaws were pried open and their mouths filled with compacted earth.

"Let the invades see what has been wrought this night," Throm said, pointing his upturned palm to the circle of the dead.

Hralda took hold of his wrist. "But let us first make sure we are far away when they do," she said. "Otherwise, naught will be wrought hereafter."

ANTOS TOOK AN IRON GLADIUS FOR HIMSELF TO REPLACE HIS bronze sword, though he carried it as a secondary, being a part of what he had been. Grola, Breht, and Flohs took a sword each, and so now, when Antos trained, there were three who joined him. With four swords left to donate, they made their way to the city closest to the pass that had allowed them through the great mountain range that divided Westmeer from the Umberlands they had fled.

Burnlock, the small city was called, in the Umber tongue. Brandonslot to those who lived there. They were cautious to approach, knowing they would look to the eyes of those who dwelled there like the wildfolk who raided their lands. For they dressed in skins and hides that suited their humble needs, sleeping in the wilds instead of attending halls. They were further uncertain how Grola and Breht might be received with their horns and hooves.

As their leader, Valris decided that Antos, still proudly wearing his Sond armor would be best received. As an empire that never reached this far, in conquest, but who had trade routes with Westmeer, he would not be seen as hostile. Though he did not speak the Nord tongue of the Westmeerians. None of them did.

When they encountered a small patrol north of Burnlock, they approached slowly and cautiously, attempting to assert some clear intention to parlay. The small group stopped at their approach, standing in leather and quilted armor under blue tabards.

"Do you speak Umber?" Antos asked, presenting his raised open palms.

One of the Westmeerian soldiers tilted his head and squinted. He said something in the local tongue, clearly not grasping Antos's words.

Antos repeated the words, slower and louder, but the soldier shook his head and shrugged. One of his companion's said something, pointing at the Sond soldier. All that could be clearly discerned was the words "Umber," and "Sond." They talked amongst themselves a moment before another soldier stepped forward, with a look of intrigue.

"Are you... speaking Umber?" the second soldier to address them asked, in their tongue.

"Yes," Antos and Valris both said, together.

"Ah," the soldier said, smiling with realization. "You're a Sond soldier, aren't you?"

"Yes," Antos said.

"Sorry, with the accent, we didn't realize you were speaking Umber," he said, with his own accent, that bent and twisted each word in its own flavor. "It's hard to understand a second tongue, in a third accent."

"Especially when you speak it in a fourth," Ethela quietly mumbled to Valris. Though, after a couple years spent with him, the group had gotten use to the way Antos spoke. They too had struggled at first.

Valris cocked an eyebrow, as she looked back to Ethela, before stepping forward. "That's my fault," she said. "My name is Valris Oakenflesh. I thought you would respond better to a fellow soldier, than people you might mistake for wildfolk."

"Ah, see, now *that* I understood," the second soldier said. "My name is Yopp. Watchman Yopp. The fact that you didn't attack us, as soon as you saw us, made us realize you weren't wildfolk. So, tell me, what's all this about?"

"We need to speak with someone in charge, at your city," she said. "We bring important news."

"What sort of news?" Watchman Yopp asked.

Valris walked around to Throm, partially opening the red canvas he was using to stow bloodied Kestrian uniforms. "The Kestrian invasion of Westmeer has begun," she warned. "These came from a scouting camp made for more men than we found there. We've come to help, however we may, and make some alliance."

Yopp nodded. "A camp on this side of the Gods' Spine," he said, concerned. He then began to talk to the first soldier in their own tongue, before turning back to Valris and Antos. "My corporal says you'd better come with us then."

BURNLOCK KEEP WAS A STONE FORT BUILT IN THE FOOTHILLS of the great mountain range. It stood in split levels, as the terrain dictated, on higher ground than the city built around it. The buildings closest to the defensive curtain wall, outside the keep, were made of stacked and mortared stones. Built tough to resist attacks when the explorers from colder places came and conquered the orcs who were once the dominant race in these parts, once called the Orclands before the men of Nordmeer renamed it 'Westmeer' and settled. Houses and other buildings, further out, were made of wood.

If there was one kingdom in Edenya who could resist the Kestrian expansion, it was Westmeer, Ethold had told his daughter on several occasions. A kingdom of orcslayers. It may have been the Edes who kept the beastly marauding tribes from crossing the great mountains, but it was the ancestors of Westmeer who settled a land no other men would dare enter. Ethela hoped he was right.

The group were led through the city, earning surprised looks from the folk who lived there. Reassured only by the local soldiers guiding them, they kept their distance. Grola, who was shy at the best of times, even amongst her own, held Breht's arm in both her hands as she kept her head low. Her long goat ears twitched nervously as she made her way through the worn grassy streets between the wooden structures in which townsfolk lived.

They were taken to a barracks by the curtain wall. Ethela was surprised that they turned short of the gates that led to the keep, where it seemed all within her group were expecting to be taken. Yopp and his corporal went ahead into the barracks, issuing some explanation in their own tongue, presumably to ease any alarm that may be raised by the visitors. They were taken through to a large room where other soldiers were ordered to clear a long bench.

They laid out the spoils of their attack as a man in armor of bronze and leather, wearing a blue cape walked in, guided by Yopp and the corporal they had met outside the city.

"This is Sir Bram Aardvelt," Yopp introduced. "He is in charge of the city's defenses."

"We're not going to speak to your lord?" Flohs asked.

"Sir Bram, is the best man to speak to, right now," Yopp assured him.

"Besides, it's not common practice to let everyone into the lord's keep the moment they first visit the city," Sir Bram said. His Umber was far clearer than Yopp's, though still carrying an accent. "I'll present whatever I learn here to him when we're done. That, I promise you." He collected a dagger off the table and examined the metal. "So, this is the metal, I've heard so much about?" He looked to those that had armed themselves with the Kestrian swords, and quietly counted the four more on the table, the eight daggers, and looked to the armor where more of the Kestrian iron was fixed to the leather. "Yopp tells me that the men you killed were on our soil?"

Valris nodded. "They have yet to finish invading our lands, but are already setting their eyes upon yours."

"More like preventing us from aiding our neighbors," Sir Bram considered. "Either way, their presence here is an official attack. Word will be sent to every lord and our king."

He looked to each of the druids before him and studied them. "Do you mean to continue attacking their scouting parties?"

"We do," Valris said.

"I am aware of your kind and, seeing as you have brought more swords than you took for yourselves, it is clear you have your own way of fighting," the commander said. "As you have a soldier with you, I assume you won't mind assistance from ours." He turned to his men and gave some order in his own tongue to the corporal who spoke no other. He then turned to Yopp. "And you, find me four volunteers amongst our ranks who speak Umber." The two men nodded and departed. He then pointed to all the armor and daggers, speaking again in his own tongue, before others collected them and took them away.

"What will you do with those?" Valris asked.

"I've ordered that they been taken to the smithy," Sir Bram said. "Every piece of that metal will be stripped from those uniforms and melted down with those daggers to make iron swords for us. In the meantime, I'll have four of our soldiers assigned to follow and aid you, wielding these Kestrian swords you gifted us. I've also sent for three rangers to see what they think of these bows," he said, picking one of them up to examine it. "But they'll definitely want to use the arrows. I can bolster your number by these seven, to aid you in raiding small parties. The goal being to bring back as much of this metal and their swords as you can. We'll turn their scouting parties into supply lines for ourselves."

"We are honored to have them," Valris said, offering her hand in the practice of wrist grabbing to which those who dwelled in cities and towns were accustomed.

Sir Bram shook her arm, in friendly agreement. "It is fitting that you be a part of this first assault upon the invaders," he said, looking to Grola and Breht. "For as I say, I have heard of your kind. Those woodland dwellers who commune with trees, take animal forms, and so on. For many counts them amongst the wildfolk, or at least once did, but we have never been attacked by them. Perhaps others will now better understand."

"So, there are our kind in your lands?" Hralda, the birdcaller, asked. "Know you of where we might find them?"

The commander shook his head. "As I say. We were never attacked by them, so we let them be. Nor have we actively sought them out. Perhaps the rangers we fetch will know more. I have heard of small settlements, or at least places of gathering in which your kind dwell, but I had never thought to look into it. Though, I'm surprised to see you driven eastwards so. For atop this Kestrian empire in the making sits their general, Etyus. I have heard rumor, word, mentions, what have you, of those who have laid eyes upon him. They say he has the strength of several men and possess other strange gifts upon which have yet to be elaborated, to my ears. But he possesses the curious feature, or so I've been told, of a small pair of horns upon his temples. Like that of a ram, they say, black and curling."

"A ram changeling?" Grola said, touching her own goat horns as she looked to Breht, the stag.

"In charge of an empire?" Breht said, shaking his antlered head. "Making war with every kingdom within reach? I could not understand how such a thing would come to pass."

"It does seem very unlike your kind," the commander said. "But that is what I have heard. Perhaps joining forces with you will offer us some advantage against him in the long run, though, if that is what he truly is."

"If he truly is one of us, then his crimes are far greater than any could hope to imagine," Valris said. "We have lost many of our kind to his soldiers. Several, close to us."

Sir Bram nodded slowly. "I'm sorry to hear that," he said. "But we will help you get revenge on as many of them as possible. At least on the ones who enter this kingdom, for now." He looked about in contemplation. "I think I can arrange accommodation here," he offered. "You'd be better staying here than at the inn. Besides, I imagine you carry no coin, anyway," he said, earning a headshake from Valris to confirm. "Well, we do have a kitchen, if you wish to eat."

"I think at least two of us would be more comfortable in the surrounding woodlands, where the trees still live and thrive," Valris said. "For the dead trees that make many of these homes, and other gathering places, have no voice. We cannot sleep in such a place."

"Well, at least let me feed you," the commander said.

Valris smiled apologetically. "Not to sound ungrateful, but that depends on what you have to eat."

"Oh, are you like the elves and eat no meat?" he asked.

"We do, but for those amongst us who inhabit the spirit of certain beasts, we refrain from eating the flesh of their kind," Valris explained. "No goat, no venison, no boar, no bear, nor birds that fly."

"All the better that you dine with us instead of the city's lord then," Sir Bram said, with an amused smile. "Beef and mutton are the only meats that make it to the barracks' kitchen. Occasionally fish or foul, but that's a weekly event at best and today is not that part of the week. A bowl of vegetable stew and chunk of bread is all I believe we can offer you here."

Valris nodded with a grateful smile.

"Good, that'll give the others time to round up those I sent them out for," the commander said, ushering them in the direction of the mess hall.

WHEN ETHELA AND HER DRUIDIC BRETHREN DEPARTED THE city, once more to the fearful looks of the townsfolk, they did so with seven more to their number. Four watchmen came, including Yopp, under the leadership of Vendel. He was much older than the others, not far from Ethela's father's age, a few years shy of sixty. Thin, but sinewy and tough, he marched with rare vigor. Of the three rangers, leadership was assumed by the oldest amongst them. Pella her name was, eager to test the Kestrian bow with which she'd been armed.

The bows were tested against rabbit and turkey, that became dinner for the party of fifteen. Hralda had no objection to turkey, having never communed with them in her capacity as bird caller. Together the group plucked and skinned their prey, made camp, and ate together, sharing stories. As they talked of loss and separation, Pella the ranger, spoke up.

"There is an encampment…" she began, while the senior watchman, Vendal, exchanged notes and pointers on fighting styles with Antos. "Well, I suppose, that's the wrong word for it. There are no tents or buildings. I suppose an enclave or gathering, perhaps."

"A grove," Ethela said, watching the watchmen and Antos teaching Flohs, Breht, and Grola.

"A grove, then," the ranger said, with a point of gratitude towards Ethela. "That does sound familiar. It's to the east, a few days. Just beyond Mangelkrans Village. At some point, when we get the chance, I can take you all there, if you'd like."

"That would be most appreciated," Valris said. "You've had dealings with them before? Are there many?"

"It's a small community, yes," she said, picking her teeth with a tiny broken turkey bone. "There must be at least a few dozen. I'm not sure, it's all within series of channels and trenches that was once a network of deep but narrow creeks before the river that fed it water was redirected and made them run dry."

"With an invading force on your doorstep, when will it even be safe to go that way?" Ethela asked, concerned they might never get a chance. "For now, it's the wrong direction."

"Kestrians have finally set foot in Westmeer," Pella said. "Word shall be sent to every city along the Gods Spine now, and word shall be sent to the king. If we find more of them encroaching upon our lands, I imagine soldiers will be sent westwards. Defensive posts set up at every pass, and possibly scouting parties of our own. When that happens, I think it'll be safe to take your there. Hopefully, by then, the Kestrians will be deterred and your nearby grove won't need…." Pella looked towards Hralda, who was sitting upright with her forearms crossed upon her chest and her eyes closed. "Is she alright?" she asked, pointing her bonepick at the eldest of the druids.

"She is communing with the birds," Throm said, seated beside his distant lover. "Seeing what they see, going where they go."

"Does she control them?" Pella asked.

"No," the large man said, with a dismissive smile. "Nor does she order them. That is not the nature of their relationship. She always describes it as asking them for sight and though they usually comply, they never stop being who they are. They do not give up control, merely yield to suggestion. It is as if she is one of their flock, though she sees though all of their eyes."

"Remarkable," Pella said, in wonder.

"I don't think they even know she's there," Ethela said. "I think they each think that her suggestions are coming from another bird, or perhaps a few, within the flock. She doesn't make them do anything, but in the end, they do as she would. Her influence is strong, though not by her design. They just become more like her. Birds fly away when people walk near, but when she is with them, they do not fly from us. I think because while she shares her mind, we seem as familiar to them as we do to her. They feel as she does towards us when she shares her mind."

Throm smiled and nodded. "That is why she must close her eyes. Not just for concentration, but because the sight goes both ways. If they see what she sees while they are flying, they will become confused and likely crash."

Ethela looked back to those who were practicing swordplay. "Flohs, on the other hand," she said, pointing to him with her thumb. "That's another story. I cannot begin to imagine what it must be like amongst the trees. No words, no thoughts. A strange sort of…knowing."

"Though he definitely controls them," Valris said. "For he makes them do things they could not do on their own."

"What can one possibly make a tree do?" Pella asked, intrigued. "They don't do anything, ever."

"Subtle things," Valris said, of her long-suffering admirer. "He can make them loose and drop their fruit when we are hungry, release acorns when we need them, drop catkins in abundance to distract pursuing creatures, and raise their roots to trip and hold enemies. He can even bend branches, not by much and not terribly fast, but sometimes when one is just a little out of reach and you need to climb it."

Pella was smiling more than seemed natural for her, as she shook her head. "Truly incredible," she said.

"Surely, you must have seen similar things in your dealings with the grove to the east," Throm said.

"I have not spent long periods of time with them, only spoken in passing," she said. "Though I have been there a few times. I've not seen any of these tree tricks you speak of, but I know there are those amongst their number who must have some relationship to the woods. For they do not cut down wood to build or burn. Like you, only making fires from that which has fallen. Sometimes building from that which has collapsed some time ago, always saving what may be uprooted in a storm if they can. I know they have shifters, though I've never seen any take their second skin. But I have watched an old man separate water from mud, into the purest I have ever tasted. I have met a seamstress who works with spiders' silk, purely because the spiders make the thread for her. I have met changelings like Breht and Grola. Some just like them, some who are more beastly, and some who are more human. I know a boy who is part lynx, though you'd barely realize it to look at him, until you watch him climb a tree. Or shake his hand, for that matter," she said, with a grin.

Valris smiled at Ethela. "I would very much love meeting them."

"And they you, I'd imagine," Pella said. "But I doubt any of them speak Umber, so I suppose this joined party might be a good opportunity to learn. What with seven native speakers to practice on."

Before Ethela could respond, Hralda gasped, as she returned to them from her trance. She blinked and looked around disoriented, as she always did after a long commune. Even though she had found her gift young, the fact that the transition still affected her so, at nearly fifty years of age, was a reminder to Ethela that shifting into the boar would never get much easier.

"What did you see?" Throm asked, as he gently massaged her arms. Easing them from their long-held position.

"None have crossed the Spine of Gods this night, but many are camped close to the pass," she said. "Beyond that, they are lying flat rock in broad paths leading eastward. As they did all the way to Sondaal."

"They are building their roads," Pella said, dusting herself off as she stood. "As great a weapon as their iron." She looked about a moment before spotting the other two rangers. "Joeb," she called to one of them, walking towards him. The two spoke a moment in their native tongue and soon he was on his way. He left, jogging back towards his city.

"Where is he going?" Valris asked.

"I have sent him to relay this news to Sir Bram," Pella explained. "He can make it there and back well before any Kestrians can march on us. Besides, he is our scout. One of the best I know. But clearly, he has nothing on Hralda. So, he'll serve better as a runner on this mission."

IT WAS TWO DAYS BEFORE MORE KESTRIAN SOLDIERS FOUND their slain scouting party. By the time Hradla saw them through the eyes of a small flock of birds, they were already filling in their field graves. As she had described it, they had seemed shaken and were ill-equipped to rebuild the camp. But they brought other supplies and, with seemingly no secondary order beyond joining those already camped there, they set up as best they could, sending a small group of men back to report to others.

"How many are camped there now?" Vendel asked. The older sergeant of the watchmen clenched a fist over the flat round pommel of the gladius by his side.

"I think twenty," Hralda said. "Twenty with the others sent away."

"Then we best attack soon," Vendel said. "They'll be bringing back more, soon enough."

"I suppose today's lessons in our tongue will have to wait," Pella said, as she signaled the other two rangers. "Otherwise, we'll all end up having to learn the Kestrian tongue."

"That is not an option for us," Valris said. "The Kestrians mean to wipe us out. Our kind, that is."

Pella furrowed her brow as they began to make their way towards the enemy camp. "Wipe you out?"

"They may be conquerors, who mean to rule over those who live in cities, sleeping in homes of dead trees and broken rock, but for those of us pledged to gods other than the old Twelve, they have only the desire to kill," Ethela said. "In the years they have spread, our kind have fast dwindled. Since they have driven the Sond forces off the mainland of Edenya, conquering all to the west, and turned their eyes southward, from where they once began, they have hunted us in the wilds because we do not follow the old faith."

"They mean to force the old faith upon us?" Vendel said, in a bitter growl. "We worship the new and honor the old. That is our way. Twelve festivals a year, not endless masses, and all that other miserable ritual." The rest of his rant sank into a low grumble as he marched a little faster, out of anger, forcing everyone else to hasten their pace.

"I think what the sergeant is trying to say," Ranger Pella said, "is that we're not going to let them come for you. Not for us. Not for anyone in this kingdom."

As with the last time, the attack took place at night. While several of the camping soldiers were sleeping. Without tents to obscure them, the rangers were free to spread out and ready their arrows. Hralda landed birds near the camp once more. This time higher, perched in the branches of nearby trees, knowing there would be arrows involved. Throm and Ethela took their second skins and became the great bear and wild boar. The pair took down the patrolling sentries, savagely ripping into them before they could draw their weapons. Ranger arrows took those tending the fire, before the watchmen and druids, armed with the swords of Kestrian iron, charged in to assault those awakening to the attack. As roots climbed to the surface of the forest floor, called upon by Flohs, tripping and impeding the soldiers' response, some got past, only to be distracted by swooping birds.

Soon, all were within the camp. The attack came fast and unrelenting. The swords that met the invaders' swords were not broken as brass would be, for they were of their own making. Though they were the most organized army the continent of Edenya had ever known, they were not ready for an attack by bird, boar, bear, iron, and root.

The dead soldiers were stripped of their armor and weapons and the camp of its supplies. All that left was what had been left the last time. A circle of naked dead holding hands with soil-filled mouths and missing hearts fed to their fire. The city-dwelling watchmen were not pleased by the practice. Clearly a savagery to their civilized sensibilities, but they did not deter nor condemn it. The rangers seemed less disgusted, or at least less shocked. Only Ranger Pella seemed to show the mildest sign of approval. Appreciating the fear it would put in the hearts of other invaders.

It wasn't until they left, that Ethela realized Varlis had been concealing a wound to her forearm.

"You're bleeding," Ethela said, shocked. "How?"

"I *was* bleeding," Valris assured her fawning lover. She tilted her head to the ranger scout. "Rijns has seen to it." She brandished her bandage. "But it was the iron sword. When it struck, merely a glancing a blow, it ignored my oakenflesh. The same arm struck that soldier's face like a battering ram breaking a door, but when the edge of his blade slid along my hardened skin, it was if slicing a fruit."

Ethela looked at her. This woman who kept her warm at night, whose love had carried her over the death of both her parents. They had fought side by side against wildfolk, bandits, and these expanding Kestrians. She was almost angry and insulted that this woman thought she could conceal the fear in her eyes. But that is where the insult ended. For Valris could see what Ethela saw and knew her ruse was broken. As they drifted from the others, falling behind as the party made for the city from which they had obtained their new allies, Valris began to speak of it.

"Oakenflesh they call me," she said. "For that is my gift. That is what I bring to battle. The might of a tree, the hardness of its…" she choked, stopping herself. "What am I, if their swords care not for this gift? How can I lead?"

"As you did before, but now more cautiously when you fight," Ethela said, grabbing her uninjured arm.

"You should have taken leadership," she said. "They all wanted that."

"Why? Will these iron swords be more merciful to me?" Ethela asked. "The bronze ones weren't? You're now vulnerable in a way I always was. As Throm always was. As all of us always were. Even my father."

"I have seen swords glance off you, when you are the boar," Valris said.

"Aye, off my hard back," Ethela said. "And that on a good day. A lucky day. Struck the right way on the only hard patch I have. You have seen the scars luckier shots have left. Arrow, sword, and spear. I must always face my enemy. But I hesitated a few nights ago when a man, who was bleeding to death on the ground, pointed one of those iron swords at me. For in that moment, I did not know if my back was made of the same magic as your oakenflesh, Oakeanflesh. I did not know if my back was truly that of a hardback leathery boar to that metal, or just some woman's pink flesh ready to split open like the skin of a plum as soon as its point touched me. I still don't know. I won't know, for sure, until I am struck. Then, if I live, I'll fight with that new knowledge."

"Wise and brave, like your father," Valris said. "Your mother, too. Are you sure you shouldn't be leader?"

"A leader should be able to yell orders to those under her,

during the battle," Ethela smirked. "Not grunt and squeal. How would you know what I was even saying? Hells, I don't even think in words, when in that shape. So, even if we could read, it's not like I could scratch them into the dirt for you with my trotters." Ethela mimed writing in the air with burled fingers.

"Your father never needed words in battle," Valris reminded her.

"No, of course not. He had a lion's roar. Even the enemy stopped what they were doing and paid attention when they heard it. Wetting and soiling themselves as they did."

They both chuckled, savoring the memory.

"I have an idea," Ethela said, quickening her pace, and Valris's as she still held her arm. She led them to Ranger Pella. "Pella, those things you wear on your forearms."

The ranger was seemingly snapped out of some trance. "Sorry what?" she said, as the words seemed to sink in before Ethela could repeat them. "Uh, vambraces?" she said, raising her left arm as her right held the belts through which several swords were sheathed, over her shoulder. "What about them?"

"The Kestrian armor has small pieces of iron fixed to sections of it. Do you think they could be melted down into flat pieces to fix to a pair of their… vambraces?"

Pella nodded. "Plated vambraces?" she asked. "They have been around a while; I think you'll find. I'm sure higher-ranking soldiers wear them." Her furrowed brow smoothed as she looked to Valris's bandaged arm and nodded, understanding the query. "But I could have our smith make some for you. Sir Bram would allow that."

"Perfect," Ethela said, looking to Valris. "Now you can commit your hands, a little less worried." She smiled at Valris, who was nodding but watching Pella.

"You seemed rather distant there, ranger," Valris said.

"Oh, sorry," Pella said, still too occupied by her distracted thoughts to explain.

Ethela gave her a nod, but watched her as the pair slunk back again. She realized the ranger was watching Flohs, and quietly pointed it out to Valris. They smiled at each other as they walked through the night.

WHEN THEY RETURNED TO THE CITY, WITH NEAR TWO DOZEN more iron swords, more arrows, more uniforms to strip of their studding, they were assigned more watchmen and rangers. Camps were also set up near the mountain gap to reinforce their number and give them somewhere to retreat. Valris was issued her iron-plated vambraces to protect and deflect.

Over the following month, their growing group ambushed and looted three more parties. The scouting squads seemed to grow in number each time, but then in turn, so did the defenders of Westmeer's border. The enemy grew more prepared and cautious. The druids led by Valris, the rangers, and watchmen, all suffered injury as night attacks inevitably became less of a surprise to the enemy. Two watchmen were lost, a ranger taken off duty indefinitely from their crippling wounds, and Breht suffered an injury that saw him limp for weeks. Though the soldier who did it was torn open by Breht's mighty antlers, Grola stayed close to him after that, refusing to let him out of her sight.

Through westbound birds, Hralda saw the Kestrians amassing numbers facing eastwards. Numbers their defensive raiding party could not hope to repel. Numbers that the armies of the Umberland kingdoms were failing to slow or sufficiently hinder. Sending the flock northwards, she reported that the defenses on the northern passes were not faring so well. To the south, the fourth pass near the coast was holding. With the regional capital not so far east from it, they were able to reinforce the town by that lowest pass. Sending birds east, as far as she could, Hralda sent them high to spy the kingdom's army marching to defend its border.

"How far?" Sergeant Vendel asked.

"Perhaps two days' march?" Hralda said. "But I have watched the Kestrians fight. Tall shields plated in their iron with spears at the ready and iron upon their heads, they walk together as one. The bronze swords of the umbers rarely make it through the advancing wall. For all our victories, I do not think the war ahead will go well."

"A grim assessment," Vendel said, screwing his face. "But an honest one, I fear."

"At the very least, our druid friends will not bode well," Ranger Pella admitted. "Perhaps it is time I took you to find the others of your kind. From there, I don't know what step could next be taken, though there are options."

"The long sight is an advantage I'd hate to lose," Vendel said, shaking his head. "But if all we'll see now is doom marching upon us, then perhaps we'd all be more comfortable going to the next fight with less certainty." He looked to the ranger. "Do it. Take them." He shook each of their hands. "Find your kind and find somewhere safe. Go as far east as you can."

Pella took Ranger Rijns with her as she left her people to guide the druids to the grove of which she spoke. In doing so, they had to leave the iron arrows behind, and those amongst the druids who carried them, gifted the iron swords, they had claimed in their first attack in this kingdom, to the watchmen. Better arming those who meant to stand against the oncoming forces.

"My gladius will stay here also," Antos said, removing

instead his bronze Sond sword to his friends' confusion. "As I wield it against those who felled the empire of my people." He handed his original sword to Breht. "You were my most promising student. I want you to carry this so that in some way, I am still protecting all of you." They all embraced him, one to two at a time, Grola the longest. "Thank you for being my family these last years, but I am a soldier first. I must do what soldiers do."

Though he was not truly one of them, he had become a part of them. They left with heavy hearts to be parted from another amongst their number. Their group ever shrinking as they found themselves slowly retreating eastward.

Hralda had sent birds ahead, the last morning they camped before reaching the grove. Though no words could be exchanged, they recognized the talents of their own kind, upon seeing the visiting birds and were ready to receive the foreign druids when they arrived. Pella translated whenever there were shortcomings in the local tongue, that she had taught her Umber friends. Amongst them, they found changelings like Breht and Grola, shifters like Ethela and Throm, callers like Hralda and Flohs, seers, and those like Valris who borrowed aspects of the elements.

An old man approached them. At first, he seemed a changeling who had become part stag like Breht with decorated antlers sprouting from his temples. But upon closer examination, they were branches, flowering small petals. A pair of sparrows sat upon one, together. As he saw Ethela looking to the birds, he smiled. "I do not influence them as the callers do," he said. "I just feed them often enough to bribe friendship out of them."

His beard hung dark green like the hanging foliage of a

willow, swaying long, down past his belly as he sat on a large rock. It was smoothed by the flow of the creek that had once been and cushioned by moss that had grown over it since.

There was an exchange of names, and they learned his was Oedyk. "Our seers say you come east in the shadow of the threat beyond the mountains," he said.

"A shadow that means to cast itself across the kingdom," Valris said. "Many of our kind have fallen to it. We came here to warn you."

Oedyk reached into a pouch by his hip. From it he brought up grains to sprinkle in his other palm, that he held up to the birds who ate from it with their tiny beaks. "Consider us warned," the old man said. "The question now is what do we do?"

"What are our options?" Valris asked. "We are new to these lands and still know too few who live in it. None, this far east."

"If fighting were an option, I doubt we'd be meeting you now, but I suspect there's more to this."

Varlis and Ethela explained what they learned of the enemy. How iron cut through bronze and even easier through the magic of druids and witches. Hralda spoke of what she saw through the birds and Pella spoke of the deeds of the druids she brought to the grove.

"There are two streams of magic from which to drink," Oedyk said, fishing more grain from his pouch for the birds in his branches. "One is nature and the other is the arcane. Those who draw upon nature make druids and witches, but those that draw from the arcane make warlocks and sorcerers."

"Every sorcerer and warlock of any value will have been called upon by the lords of the regions and king," Ranger Pella said. "We cannot call upon them for aid."

"I have seen those I suspect to be sorcerers amongst the

Kestrian armies," Hralda reminded them. "So, their kind will indeed be in great demand."

"That is why we must consult Kai Jirren," Oedyk said. "For his kind are forbidden by the gods themselves to interfere directly in the wars of men. They have watched empires rise and fall and seen entire peoples wiped out in uprisings and conquests."

"Would your plight seem any different to a wizard now?" Pella asked.

"He will not join us in battle, nor summon an army from beyond, on our behalf," the old man said, "but the least we can do is seek his counsel."

"Where can this wizard be found?" Ethlea asked.

"The wizard of Westmeer has two towers within the kingdom. His old tower in the northern region, and the west tower of the city of Twinspire, farther to the east," the old man said. "Though the former is little more than a ruin he uses as a library, now, there is some chance of him being found in either."

"Then I recommend Twinspire, being the furthest from danger," Ranger Pella suggested. "By the time we got to the north one, Kestrian forces could be there waiting for us, if our own soldiers do not succeed in holding them back from the northern passes."

"Very well," the old man said. "It will take a while to get everyone moving, and to wait for those of us who are out in wilds to return. Until then, you are more than welcome to stay amongst us, and tell us of yourselves."

———

THE SUNKEN GROVE ACCEPTED THEIR NEW COMPANIONS FROM across the mountains. A warm and welcoming community, they swapped tales and history and ate together. Ethela did much to keep Ranger Rijns occupied during their stay. Primarily improving her and Valris's local tongue, but also to leave Ranger Pella free to occupy Flohs's time. The rugged ranger's attention served well to distract the Earthenheart from his long-held affections for Valris.

"It is a kind thing you are doing," Valris gently whispered, huddled with Ethela in a small sleeping burrow that was dug beneath the dry bank. "Clearing a path for that huntress."

"Flohs has saved my life so many times," Ethela said. "I feel guilty having what he wants."

"Though, I do not know how long they might have together," Valris said, concerned.

"None of us do. That is why it is important to take what you can, as soon as you can, so that you have it all the longer."

"For as long as you can hold it," Valris said, pressing against Ethela's back. She tightened her arms, already wrapped around her. "And that is why I hold you as much as I can, whenever I can. If it were up to me, that is all I would do."

"That is *all* you would do?" Ethela asked.

"In one form or another," Valris whispered, kissing the back of her neck.

When dawn came, they led the large group east under Pella's direction. For two weeks they walked, passing by towns and cities, staying in none. They camped outside, with too large a group to impose upon any barracks. Pella sent Ranger Rijns in to get news, and fetch what provisions they could from their fellow rangers, supplemented by passing waves of soldiers marching west to defend the border. Marching to war.

They received word that Kestrian ships were sighted off the north and south coast patrolling the surrounding waters of Westmeer. Though there was at least no word of landing parties, tensions were rising in every part of the kingdom.

In the second week of travel, they saw a large party traveling west but passing too far north to greet. From the heraldry and armor, Ranger Pella was certain it was Prince Aurin Noordgaard himself leading them. She and Rijns were quite excited. Honored just to have seen him. Such hierarchal extremes were so foreign a concept to the druids, though they lived upon lands owned in name by such figures.

"If such elation and splendor were afforded *our* leaders, I might not have stepped aside," Ethela whispered to Valris.

"I wonder if he fights with a sword made of gold?" Valris quietly joked.

Upon reaching the city of Twinspire, a pair of towers around which the city was built in encircling layers, broadest at the base where they met, the large party camped outside once more. In the shadow of the two great structures upon which both moons were represented by a great disc sat upon the east tower and a crescent upon the west. Rangers Pella and Rijns entered the city the evening they arrived, to climb the west tower to seek audience with the wizard known to dwell there.

A significant climb, presumed wait, and downward return journey, the pair were gone some time before they returned to the camp. When they did, it was late.

"He will see us all tomorrow," she informed them.

Oedyk looked up to the east tower. "That does seem a hefty climb," he said, rubbing his lower back as if he'd already made half the journey.

Ethela smiled when she heard him and pointed to the birds in one of the branches growing from his head. "Perhaps you can have your little friends fetch more birds to land in your branches and flap furiously to take some of the weight."

The old man laughed. "It's just shame that amongst the shifters I know, there's large cats, a bull, a red deer, a reindeer, and now a bear and a boar, but none amongst you had the foresight to become a horse."

Ethela laughed.

———

IT WAS A SLOW CLIMB WITH OEDYK, OTHER ELDERLY AMONGST the grove, and children of various ages. The guards at the south gate of the city were alarmed by the number, and those within that number that exhibited unusual features, to the eyes of those who lived within high walls. Though, with a wizard living in their city, training others in magic, the city guards had most likely become accustomed to magic being represented purely by men and women in long fine robes.

The wizard was not what Ethela had expected. In place of a beard like Oedyk's, his medium one grew down to his collar and from only around his mouth, black like his shoulder-length hair, and peppered with grey. Adorned in orange robes, he wore a longsword by his side and carried a long, lacquered staff with three brass rings placed evenly upon its length with a round pommel at one end and a crescent at the other.

Too numerous to be contained within the level of the tower in which they were greeted, the grove of druids they had brought spilled out into the surrounding balcony path, overlooking the city. Sorcerers studying under the wizard made space for them, curious to witness the unusual gathering.

"I have watched the might of the Kestrians grow under this General Etyus," Kai Jirren said. "As have my fellow wizards; Kai Methynial as they conquered westward, Kai Ghoruus as they returned to now take the lands south of where they once began. Now, as they set their eyes upon the great kingdom of Westmeer, I am forced to watch their expansion, forbidden from interfering."

"They say this Etyus has the horns of a ram," Ethela remarked. "If he is a changeling, it is hard to believe he would threaten his own kind so."

"Not the horns of a ram," the wizard said. "More like the horns of a black dragon. He is not one of your kind. But he is also not a Kestrian, truly. It would not be on his orders that your kind are hunted, but the intolerant ethos of a misguided tribe who grew too strong. One who cleverly adopted one such as Etyus as their military leader. But it is the misguided and outdated faith of these people, that hunts you. Those who otherwise displayed innovation in discovering the power of paved roads and the might of iron, but not the strength of harmony." He stepped towards a window of his high tower with one hand behind his back, and the other resting on his staff. "I cannot predict how far this power will spread, nor predict a true haven from their expansion. Wherever you venture across the Middle Sea, will they not someday follow? The forests of Dantos or Ortalyn? The hot jungles or deserts of Heruud? Perhaps even the icy cold of Craguhr. There is only one place where you would truly be out of their reach."

"Where?" Valris asked.

The wizard looked at each of them. "Perhaps the Endless Wilds of Etherius."

All else looked to the wizard as if he had gone mad.

"The realm of Brechor?" Ethela asked? "I think, in their own way, that is already where the Kestrians mean to send us, through violence."

The wizard shrugged. "If that is the path you would prefer," he said. "But I could grant you passage. You could go there now, alive. Escape this world as many of the orcs once did when men came to claim this kingdom once called the

Orclands. Out there," he said, pointing westward, "is the grey dawn of your doom. The age of iron is upon us. When the next empire comes, they will not go back to bronze or copper, stone or wood. Your time has come to leave this world. I will be sad to see your kind gone, but glad to know I could save you in my own way."

"To go where we go when we die?" Throm scoffed, confused. "Are we not better off then to die fighting to keep what is ours?"

"When *you* die…" the wizard stopped himself, from finishing his retaliatory explanation, with a sigh of defeat. Some wisdom to be withheld, he nearly spilled for ears that were not meant to hear it. "I'm offering you a rare gift, that I cannot make you understand. Go then. Die from a dozen spears plunging into your bearskin. Your meat roasted by hungry soldiers who believe you to be nothing more than a beast trained to attack. At the very least left to rot on the field of battle to be picked by crows with no prayer to guide you in the beyond."

"Alright," Throm said, apologetically raising his hands in surrender at the wizard's tone.

"We do appreciate this great gesture, Kai Jirren," Valris said, placating the wizard.

"For those who do wish to go this way, know that there is a price," the wizard said. "There must always be a trade. As there is some urgency to your required departure, I cannot send you on some quest I might a warrior who comes to me for some enchantment. So, who will bear the burden of trade for all the souls I send through?"

Ranger Pella stepped forward, daunted. "As one who has no claim to their destination, I suppose that leaves me," she said, stroking her chin in worried contemplation. "What task would you impose upon me for their safe passage to the realms beyond?"

The wizard walked towards her, assessing her with his eyes. "That's very noble of you," he said, inquisitively.

"Yeah, well, what can I say," she said, looking towards Flohs, with whom she had grown close. "Without some of them, I would not have enjoyed the victories against our enemies that I have. I will gladly take whatever debt is owed, if it means saving them." She then pointed to Ranger Rijns. "And I can probably order him to help me, so there's that."

Rijns shook his head but smiled. "Of course," the scout committed.

"Very well," the wizard said. "Then I charge you with this task. Go and search the kingdom for more of their kind. All, if you can track them down. Bring them to me, so that I may save as many as we may."

Pella huffed in disbelief. A surprised smile creeped across her face as she looked up to the tall figure before her. This powerful immortal who walks amongst men, using his pact of conditional assistance to assist even further. "I accept this task," she said, proudly. "I shall query every ranger barracks in each city and every ranger fort in the wilds."

"That won't be enough," Flohs said. "You'll need more insight than the luck of other rangers who crossed paths with other groves. You'll need to know what the trees do. I shall have to stay and aid you."

Pella seemed uncertain how to respond. It was no secret that she would be loath to farewell him, but nor would she be comfortable depriving him of his escape. "I don't know if…"

"You needn't know anything other than the fact that I will help you in this," he insisted.

"Of course, you'd have more success if you knew what the birds could see," Hralda said, reluctantly.

"If you stay, I stay," Throm told the birdcaller.

"No," she said, putting her hand on his chest. "The others will need you on the other side."

"They'll need *you* on the other side," he said.

"If there are even any birds there to share their sight," Hradla dismissed.

"If not the birds, your wisdom," he argued.

Hralda slowly shook her head. "If they need anything, it's a great bear to protect them," she said, caressing his strong jaw. "Go, and I will follow when we can find no more to send through."

"And if the Kestrians come for you when you are too far from this place?"

"Then I will come to you the other way, but I will find you again." Hralda grabbed his face with both hands and passionately kissed him. "Go," she said with a sad smile.

The wizard raised his staff in both hands, about to point it, before hesitating. "When you step into the other side, do not step back through. If you change your mind, do so on this side and face your fate. Attempt to pass back, and that will be the end of you. Find somewhere nearby, on the other side, to gather and wait. Somewhere you can hide. I will send one of my pupils to give you the rest of your instructions, to guide you and to explain how things work. There is a long journey ahead, but you will not be safe to move or engage anything you find there until I send word to the contrary. Understood?" he asked, but did not seem to wait for an answer.

The wizard held the crescent end of his staff towards the gathered throng of druids filling the level of his temple. He closed his eyes and muttered words beneath his breath, making small circles as if stirring the air. Soon the air around it began to bend and twirl, rippling with a purple glow that seemed to burn the very fabric of reality. A silver pool began to form before them like a metallic pond of quicksilver, somehow on its side. Once satisfied at its presence, Kai Jirren gently dipped the crescent end of his staff into it and slowly pulled down, stretching it down into a large oval. The silver portal, framed by purple energy, stretched about four feet in height, floating a foot off the floor.

Valris and Ethela stood back as they watched their new expanded grove duck and pass through the rippling silver portal, one by one, until only they, Grola, Breht, and Throm were left of those who were about to pass through to the other side. Grola and Breht quickly embraced Hralda, Flohs, and the ranger. Hastened by the wizard clearing his throat, they left with an exchanged nod.

"No time for speeches, it seems," Hralda said. She kissed Throm and sent him through, before kissing Valris and Ethela on their foreheads. "Oakenflesh and boar, I charge you with keeping that bear I love safe for me."

"Till we meet again," Valris said to the others, as she took Ethela by the hand.

The first of the last, Ethela realized as she watched her lover slip through the fluidic reflective gateway. Her hand slipping loose, yanked out of her grasp as she vanished. Their kind were leaving the world, most likely forever. There were no final words she could think of to say that could do the moment justice, nor the time to think of them. A defeat *and* a victory, she merely smiled at her remaining friends before stepping into the unknown.

ABOUT THE PUBLISHER

Visit our website to learn more about how to submit your work for publication.

www.dragonsoulpress.com

facebook.com/dragonsoulpress

twitter.com/dragonsoulpress

instagram.com/dragon_soul_press

pinterest.com/dragonsoulpress

youtube.com/DragonSoul_Press

Made in the USA
Las Vegas, NV
22 April 2021